Afterthoughts

A collection of short stories
by the Alaska writing group
The Life Partners

ISBN: 978-0-578-53624-8
Lens&Pens Publications

For Derek and Peter.

CONTENTS

FOREWORD

The best thing I ever did in college was take a writing workshop class. Not just because that is where I met my husband but because I found a whole community of writers to be a part of. Even after the class ended, our professor, Dave, was crazy enough to invite us all to continue meeting once a week at his house. We took him up on that offer.

Even now that more than a decade has passed and life has shuffled us all across the world, the writers in these pages remain some of the best people I have ever known. Everyone in this book is dear to my heart, and I am so excited to see a representation of each of our work finally collected together. I want to thank Skeeter for suggesting this adventure and making it happen. As well as Trevor for all his editing and patience.

The first and last stories in this collection are particularly special. Two of our most passionate and talented writer's passed away much too soon, but we wanted their work to be presented here in remembrance. Peter's story is funny and thoughtful, just like he was. And while Derek's story stands brilliantly on its own, it was originally intend as part of a whole collection of stories in one universe. I take comfort in knowing that, in this volume at least, we can all be together again.

~Cheyenne Morse

MEGALOPOLIS'S FINEST

DEREK CHIVERS

The name's Murphy—Sergeant Ryan Murphy, MPD. It's four thirty-six a.m. in Megalopolis, and I'm working graveyard with a rookie. Lucky me, eh? In case it doesn't come across clearly enough in print, that's a rhetorical question. Plus it's sarcasm. Working the graveyard shift in this city is pretty much the shit end of the stick. In fact, it's more like shit that's fallen off the shit end of the stick—making it just plain shit. And don't think for a second I'm exaggerating.

The thing about Megalopolis is that it has a draw for certain types. You know how extremely avid golfers tend to live near golf courses? Picture that only with violent crazies. I'm not sure what the golf course is in the metaphor, but they're drawn here like flies to—shit.

Have you ever heard that big cities attract big criminals? Well, Megalopolis is the biggest. There's nothing out of the ordinary about our paved streets, brick buildings, traffic lights, and rail lines. It's less than a tenth of a percent of its population that makes Megalopolis so anomalous. But with fifteen million people and gaining since the last census, even half a tenth of a percent is entirely too much.

Anyway—graveyard shift sucks.

Before we had schedule rotations, graves served as sort of a proving ground for fresh MPD recruits. Things worked out just fine that way for a while too. If you lived long enough working graves, you got a raise and moved to days, where things are much less likely—though still fairly probable—to go to hell.

That's how I got my stripes. And I'm not sure if it's tougher out here these days or the kids are just softer, but it seems like fewer and fewer recruits stick around long enough to make it to day shift.

It's not through lack of trying. These kids think they can take on the world. You know the type—bright eyed and bushy tailed, optimistic to a fault, and thinking they're going to come to the big city, join the force, and "make a difference."

Well, the only difference any recruit has made lately is a change in the way we assign duty shifts. That and an uptick for the workload at the morgue. Captains don't want to put proven lieutenants and sergeants on the street any more than any of us—who've already earned our keep—want to be there. But after the second consecutive batch of recruits all died of various atypical causes in one month, a change in policy wasn't all that surprising.

But the atypical trends toward the typical in our fair city. A recent newspaper article stated that the most likely cause of premature death in Megalopolis is contusion—including impact, trampling, compression, and the odd powderization—followed closely by dismemberment. For comparison, drunk driving didn't make the top ten. I suspect death by particle weapon might have ranked fairly high on the list if it didn't eradicate every cell of a victim's body.

From what I hear, it can be hell to get insurance to pay out on these sorts of claims.

So standard operating practice now is to pair a seasoned officer up with every piece of fresh meat out of the academy. That means each and every vet has to rotate through graveyard shift at least two weeks a year.

Personally, I don't think they pay enough for this shit, but there's always more fresh meat for the grinder. In Megalopolis, nobody's indispensable. At least I've got my stripes and an E-5 pay grade.

The top brass knows well enough that none of us will quit. It's not like anyone's ever safe in this city, anyway—at least as cops we can sometimes shoot back. But not even that keeps us protected, realistically. My cousin Bill was a cop, and kind of a hero to me when I was growing up. He was packing heat when he was riding the train to work on the day Infernus melted the G Line to the track. One minute you're on your way to work—la-di-da—the next minute the train car goes molten and begins to collapse in on itself with you inside. Who can predict that kind of shit? Now, all the above-ground train lines have heat shields. Reactionary tactics—it's all we know.

My new partner on patrol tonight is about as green as they come. His name's Ben Finn—two weeks out of the academy, and he's ready to save the world. It's the start of my second week on graves and his first night on patrol.

Never mind trying to caution him about the fate of my last partner, interred just two days ago. They never listen. They're going to be smarter than that, quicker than that. They're not going to get irradiated, mauled by ligers, stuck with poison darts, or crushed by mechanical claws. They're fucking invincible, right? Who the hell am I to say otherwise?

What they always fail realize is this isn't my first dance.

We've got car twenty-five tonight, and Finn's riding shotgun. We're patrolling West Seventy-Eighth Avenue, which is as far as I can—in good conscience—keep us from the danger zones. There's not a hospital, medical lab, radio tower, jeweler, power plant, bank, or anything else I would classify as a point of interest within a ten-block radius.

The traffic light ahead turns red, and I shift my foot on the pedals. The patrol car rolls to a stop, and Finn turns to me with that dumb-shit expectant look. I know what he's about to say, down to the letter.

"Think we'll see any action tonight, Sergeant?"

I try to make my disapproval obvious. I utter a harsh sigh and cast him a cursory sideways glance. The light turns green. I drum my fingers once on the wheel, then twice.

"Sergeant Murphy, sir?" I don't answer. "Um, sir? The light's green."

I try to address the kid with patience and understanding, but fail miserably. The tone in my voice is robbed of any such humanizing qualities by the repetitive nature of the statement coming to my lips. I'm about to throw the same ineffective lines at another walking corpse. "I can see the fucking light, Finn. I'm not the one who's having problems seeing things here. It's you." I can feel the springs of my precautionary monologue winding up, priming.

"Sir?"

"Let me ask you something—do you have a wife, Finn?"

"No, sir."

"Girlfriend?"

"No, Sir."

"How about a mother, Finn? You've got one of those, right?"

"Yes, sir, I do." The kid kind of chuckles.

"Don't you fucking laugh at me, Finn!" I'm shouting at him, making a point to fling a little spittle from my lips as I over-emphasize my f's. The kid is shocked, and that's a good thing. "This job is no joke, shit for brains!" I lower my voice and compose myself. "Listen to me. I don't know you from Adam, but I've known dozens of kids like you—so many I'm surprised I bother to remember your fucking names. I had a partner last week named Charlie, but the one before him?" I pause and shrug for emphasis. "As for your mother—I'm sure she wants to see you again, and I'm trying desperately to accommodate her right now. Fuck's sake, Finn, the last thing on earth you want to see tonight is some action! You think this—"

Suddenly, the night erupts into a fury of noise and light, cutting me short. Five small, cigar-shaped, shiny silver vehicles scream through the intersection in pursuit of an armored van. They don't appear to have any wheels, and they're much too small to fit a person inside. A new model, if I'm not mistaken.

The van careens back and forth across the road, covered in what appear to be basketball-sized metal spiders.

The vehicles are lobbing some kind of bombs at the van. Each projectile pops with a brilliant blue flash and rocks the van on its wheels, causing the driver to correct, resulting in its erratic trajectory.

"Oh shit," I moan. It's much more despair than surprise. Before I can stop him, Finn has grabbed the handset and is calling it in to base.

"Twenty-five to base fifty!" The eagerness in his voice is unrestrained. He's looking at me with his eyes wide, holding the radio in his left hand and pumping his right fist excitedly in a punching motion.

The radio crackles hesitantly. "Base fifty. Come back twenty-five."

"This is Officer Benjamin Finn. We've got an attempted five-oh-three, a five-ten, a five-ninety-four, and a—uh—" Finn looks to me questioningly. Then I see the recollection dawn on his face. "A six-oh-four! Eastbound on Broadview!"

"Ten-four, twenty-five." Then, "A six-oh-four? Throwing missiles? Uh—Ten-oh, twenty-five. Proceed with caution." I snatch the handset from Finn and give him a look of vehement disapproval.

"Ten-four, base fifty. Twenty-five in pursuit." I pause, then bark into the handset, "Eleven-ninety-nine. Twenty-five requesting backup." The fact that no one will respond to my call is a given. Hell, half the guys on the force would look the other way and never even call this shit in to dispatch in the first place. Especially if they know what those fucking spiders mean—and I do.

Snapping the radio handset back into its cradle, I turn to the fresh meat. "Nice job, Finn. Glad you were paying attention back there while I was trying to tell you how to survive your first day." I flip on the lights and siren in one motion and floor the gas pedal—smoking tires and breaking traction—taking the patrol car sideways through the intersection before straightening out eastbound in pursuit of guaranteed trouble.

By the time we catch up, the van has been tipped onto its driver's side and skidded into a brick wall where the road makes a ninety-degree turn. The five vehicles that had been chasing it down are all nearby, hovering inches off the ground. I slam on the brakes, jerk the steering wheel to the right, and bring us to a screeching halt perpendicular to the van. I kill the lights and siren.

Now I see at least twice the number of metallic spiders that were clinging to the van when it passed, and they're all trying to pry their way through the van's armor. A small drill extends from the underside of one and begins to tap the passenger-side door lock.

There are no doors or windows on the silver vehicles—I already know—but more spiders seem to be emerging from holes in their roofs.

"Well, Finn?" I gesture toward the van. "Here's your action. Got a plan?"

Rather than answer my question, the kid jumps out of the patrol car's passenger door, drawing his weapon and shouting, "Freeze!" I don't think he has the slightest clue who he's ordering to stop doing what.

"Finn, no." I'm deadpan, hardly attempting to dissuade him. I know it's no use. His blood's boiling now. I lean over and close Finn's door behind him—fuck if I'm going to let those things just climb right into the car.

While the spiders continue to pick, pry, and drill at the van, Finn takes aim and fires at the spider drilling into the passenger-side door lock. What a dumbshit. It's a decent shot, though, for all the good it will do him. I hear a dull metallic *plank* as it bounces harmlessly off the spider's metal body, followed almost simultaneously by a dry crunch and *pew* as the bullet's ricochet strikes brick.

I wonder if Finn's got a plan B, but it's obvious that he doesn't. He begins to visibly panic as the menacing metal constructs turn their eyeless attention in his direction and begin a slow advance. He manages to squeeze off two or three more well-aimed shots. Amazingly, one shot knocks a leg off of one of the spiders—I can't say I'd ever seen that before.

Then they pounce. The first spider gets a hold of Finn's gun hand. The weight and force of its impact spins him clockwise. Another spider lands on the back of his leg and digs in. The pointed legs of the spiders pierce like blades. I know, because I've felt them before. I reach up and scratch at my shoulder and the scar tissue beneath my uniform.

He's screaming, but I really don't feel all that guilty. You may think I'm heartless, but it's not like I've never seen this before. I tried to warn him. They never listen.

Finn squeezes off a few more wild rounds, before the spider attached to his hand applies enough pressure to force him to drop the pistol. I swear I can hear a cracking noise, even from inside the patrol car. Finn falls to his knees, and a third spider seizes his free arm. He is pulled to the ground by the weight of a fourth and fifth spider crawling onto his chest, soon joined by three more on his legs. Nice knowing you, kid. Then suddenly, just when I expect the spiders to rip him apart, they stop and simply hold him down.

This can't be good.

A booming, electronically amplified voice echoes from the air above.

"Who dares attempt to thwart the machinations of Dr. Terror-Achnid?"

The sky fills with smoke, pierced by the light and roar of retro-boosters, as a terrifying persona descends into view. It has the torso of a man—spindly arms crossed across the flat pectorals of an intellectual. He wears an extremely rugged, white button-flap lab coat and a maniacal grin. White and grey wiry, unkempt hair crowns a gaunt face, which is defined best by its large, beak-like proboscis. Behind a pair of goggles suited to motorcyclists or open-cockpit pilots sit wild, wide-open, accusative eyes.

If nothing else about this man inspires fear, there is his lower half. Dr. Terror-Achnid's torso sits atop the giant mechanical prosoma and abdomen of a spider. Still descending, retro rockets glow bright blue at the tip of each of his eight outstretched limbs, which span roughly twelve feet across.

About four feet from the ground, the rockets cut thrust. The immense half-mechanical man smashes into the ground with a colossal impact. The concussion is strong enough to shake the patrol car. His lower half easily distributes the force of the impact by using its eight long legs as shock absorbers, but the concrete walkway beneath him splinters and buckles. He bobs slightly upon impact, then his legs straighten, lofting him to his fully enhanced ten-and-a-half-foot height. He uncrosses his arms and shakes a fist triumphantly.

"Finally, I have you trapped in my web of terror, Blitz—" The man-robot-spider stops midsentence and tilts his head inquisitively. He flips a switch near where his hips should be. "You're not him," he says, rather matter-of-factly, in a now unamplified voice.

"I'm just a cop!" Finn screams. He's obviously in tremendous pain but attempting to retain a shred of dignity.

"Just a cop. Great! What the hell were you doing trying to stop my minions? What do you have, a death wish?"

"I'm sorry! God, I'm so sorry!" Finn is crying now. So much for dignity.

"Sorry? Sorry? Sorry doesn't replace my wasted time—I just flew here from downtown! Do you have any idea how much enriched jet fuel costs?" Then, almost as an aside, "Damn it—an incredible entrance totally wasted!"

I haven't moved yet from my seat in the patrol car. Just because I survived being caught in this guy's crossfire once doesn't mean I'm chomping at the bit for a second opportunity. These things go south quick. I'm eying the pump-action twelve-gauge mounted between the seats, knowing that the police-issue slugs can pierce the small spiders' armor. I look back out to the street where Finn is pinned down, writhing in agony.

"Minions," The doctor screeches, "release him!" I breathe a sigh of relief. "Wait—on second thought—"

Shit.

I snatch the shotgun from its cradle and open my door. I pump the action quickly, loading a shell into the chamber. Standing behind the patrol car door, I level the gun at the closest target and get ready to piss my life away for a kid I just met.

I never married. I couldn't justify it in this line of work. I'm just another replaceable cog in the machinery that drives Megalopolis, and I don't want to leave a trail of broken hearts when my time comes. My routine for the past several years has been nothing but whiskey on rocks, one-night stands, and watching kids die. It's enough to hollow anyone out. I suppose that's why I'm not troubled by the prospect of dying now. I feel numb to the entire concept. Still, I'm usually more about saving my own skin than anything or anyone else. In this town, you have to be.

I'm having a vision, though. I'm seeing this kid, Finn, scared off the force by this experience. I'm seeing him give up on *making a difference*, and moving out to the country, where there are no loonies in costumes trying to make names for themselves. I see Finn settle down, get married, and have a whole litter of little Finns.

It's probably just my over-active imagination, but I decide I have to act. I have to think about something beside myself and my next drink for once.

"Hey, asshole," I shout. I have no idea what I could possibly say to it follow up, but it feels right, and it's enough to draw the doctor's attention. He snaps his head in my direction and almost doesn't see the city bus hurtling out of the sky directly toward him.

Dr. Terror-Achnid does see the bus, though. The jets on his spider legs rocket him fifty feet to the right, out of the bus's path, with lightning speed. I watch in horror as the bus slams with incredible force into the armored van, quite probably killing the driver inside. For a moment, the wreckage of the bus stands straight out at its angle of impact—looking like a modernist, surreal tower of Pisa—before it begins to tip slowly over in the direction of Finn, still trapped beneath the metal spiders.

"I thought you might show your face here tonight!" Doctor Terror-Achnid shouts into the sky. He's apparently taken the time to turn his amplifier back on. "Don't you realize I can't be stopped?" He shakes one black-gloved fist as a familiar figure swathed in tan and red descends into view.

I watch helplessly as the bus crashes to the ground between Finn and me, blocking my view of my imperiled partner.

A response comes from the sky: "Terror-Achnid, your reign of terror ends tonight!" Arms crossed imposingly, bright red cape trailing behind him in the night breeze, Blitzkrieg has arrived.

I doubt anyone has ever had the nerve to tell Blitzkrieg that his

German Imperial cuirassier helmet, First World War regalia, and Second World War alias don't mesh—or that there were probably much better personas for a superhuman to adopt than one with racist and fascist overtones.

Honestly, it never seems that important when he's saving your ass.

"Minions, attack!" Dr. Terror-Achnid is practically frothing at the mouth as the jets the ends of his legs fire up, lifting him into the air—slowly at first, then with ever increasing speed. I glance up to see a number of the small metal spiders lifting off from the other side of the bus—perfect scale miniatures of the Doctor, sans human torso. I remember vaguely that I'd been able to take out one of those spiders once, with a perfect shotgun blast to the place where the two tagmata—the thin joint between prosoma and abdomen—join.

I break cover as the doctor and his minions rise into the air. I run around the mangled city bus to where Finn lies wounded on the ground. He's bleeding a lot from the leg, and his gun hand appears to be crushed—it's questionable if he'll ever use it again—but for the most part, he seems amazingly intact.

The sound of a plasma inversion cannon pierces the night—quite unnerving if you've never heard one before. It sounds a bit like someone's tearing a hole in reality, if that makes any sense.

"Give up now, villain! You shall not succeed—evil never triumphs!" Blitzkrieg booms from somewhere above in his ridiculously thick German accent. As if to accentuate his point, there is a loud clapping noise, and three of the doctor's minions fall mangled to the ground nearby.

"Why won't you die?" is the screeched reply, followed immediately by a loud clash of metal. The night is lit at random intervals by blue, purple, and red flashes, blossoming with deadly brilliance overhead.

"Ben, are you awake?" I'm touching him lightly on different parts of his body, trying to see if there's any internal damage. I'm going to have to move him, but I'm not excited about the prospect.

"Ryan? I thought you were going to let me die."

"So did I, and you would have deserved it too. Still feeling brave, hero?"

"No, sir."

I drag the kid back to the patrol car amidst a rain of sparks and debris. I get Finn into the back seat and turn back to the armored van. The driver could still be alive. Overhead, the clash of supervillain and superhero is in full swing. I take three strides toward the van before Dr. Terror-Achnid is slammed with astounding force into a nearby brown brick building, which comes apart like a child's set of construction bricks. The cascading avalanche of stone and mortar buries the armored van—its flow is only stopped short by the mass of the city bus.

I don't even have time to curse for the poor son of a bitch who's just been buried in his van before the doctor bursts out of the rubble. He's firing six leg-jets and gripping the armored van with the last two—hauling it into the air with him. He's laughing insanely at Blitzkrieg, who has fallen to the sidewalk, seemingly exhausted.

Without considering the consequences, I raise my shotgun and aim it at the small crux between Dr. Terror-Achnid's mechanical body's segments and fire.

For a moment, I don't think anything's happened. The gun sounds loudly and kicks hard against my shoulder, but the doctor is still ascending, cackling and shaking his fists triumphantly. Then, a shower of multicolored sparks descend like fireworks as first one, then three of the leg-jets flash, flicker, and expire.

The Doctor's face takes on the look of a man who's teetering on the edge of losing balance; his arms instinctively dart out to his sides like a tightrope walker. Three jets are apparently not enough to keep him aloft. He begins to drift steadily downward. He drops the armored van from a height of perhaps thirty feet onto the pile of rubble below, which seems to almost cushion the blow. The van slides a short distance, plowing up a small pile of bricks, then stops.

The jets on Terror-Achnid's remaining two legs, which had been gripping the van, fire up. All five functioning legs flail, searching for the adequate compensatory positions.

The doctor registers me and grimaces in my direction, pointing an index finger menacingly, but Blitzkrieg has begun to compose himself, and Dr. Terror-Achnid is forced to beat a hasty retreat into the night sky, which now shows the first promising traces of dawn's first light.

I'm just beginning to realize that I might have single-handedly turned the tide in a battle of supers when I'm approached by Blitzkrieg himself.

He's a lot shorter in person.

I actually have to look down to meet his gaze, and I'm suddenly overcome with the desire to laugh out loud at his ridiculous pointy cuirassier and bushy moustache. I stifle the urge, knowing he possesses the strength of ten thousand men.

"Citizen." He looks me up and down as if assessing my worth.

"Murphy, Sergeant Ryan Murphy."

"Well, Murphy," Blitzkrieg starts, and I ready myself for some well-deserved praise, "That was some incredibly irresponsible behavior."

"Wha—"

"Who authorized you to fire on Terror-Achnid?"

"I'm a police sergeant!"

"The Heroes Council did not authorize use of deadly force. He was to be subdued. Do you have any idea what a pain it is to document an unauthorized ballistic discharge? You'll be lucky if the Villains Guild doesn't file a motion to have you stripped of rank and suspended from the force!"

I'm having a really hard time wrapping my head around what I'm being told.

Suddenly, I remember the armored van. Without responding to Blitzkrieg, I make a mad dash to the spot where the van came to rest. I can hear someone moaning inside.

"Blitzkrieg, help him!"

The hero strolls over nonchalantly to where I'm pulling at the door to the van with every bit of strength I have left. He reaches out and peels the steel apart as if opening a paperback novel.

"He'll live. His spine is intact, and he's safe to move," he tells me.

"How do you know that?"

"I know things," he says and then begins to levitate, slowly gaining altitude.

"But he's hurt bad, and my partner's injured too! Can't you get these men to a hospital?" The hero hesitates, briefly halting his ascension to respond.

"I'm not an ambulance," he says curtly. Then, after a pause, he clarifies, "Give a man a fish, you know? Learn to help yourself, Sergeant Murphy. Anything beyond your control, consider fate." Then the squat, mismatched German rises rapidly into the air and disappears in a flourish of crimson cape.

Somehow, I manage to get the armored car driver back to my patrol car and into the back seat with Finn, who's passed out.

I pluck the radio handset from the dash. "Twenty-five to base fifty."

"Base fifty. Come back twenty-five."

"Inbound to Mercy Hospital: one officer, one civilian, both code thirty."

"Ten-four, twenty-five. Glad to hear you're still with us."

"Thanks fifty. Ten-twenty-six."

On the drive to Mercy, I race down deserted streets flashing my cherries, no siren. I need the quiet for contemplation. Blitzkrieg's words weigh heavily on me. I know I've been putting my own needs above everyone else's by allowing the heroes to clean up my city. I've always felt it was pointless to involve myself in those battles—that it was the heroes' job—but what is a police officer if not a common man's hero?

Then I remember Blitzkrieg's admonishment for involving myself in his affairs, and his cryptic comments about a Heroes Council and a Villains Guild. I can't believe there's a bureaucracy of superhumans. Did he seriously complain about paperwork?

The only conclusion I reach is that I can only do what I can do, and I shouldn't concern myself with things that don't concern me. Anything beyond your control, consider fate—isn't that what he'd said?

I was, however, beginning to develop a new concept of what was within my control.

I wonder if my vision about Finn will hold true or if he'll end up emboldened by the experience. I wonder if they'll assign me another piece of fresh meat to patrol with for my last six nights of graveyards. I wonder if I'll cross paths with another costumed loony in the meantime or if Dr. Terror-Achnid will be able to place a name with my face—a face he's now seen twice. Have I made my own archnemesis?

But soon enough, I begin to earnestly anticipate my next glass of whiskey and next session of rough, emotionless sex.

Megalopolis wasn't built in a day.

MUSEUM

MEG HELLENTHAL

Next to the windows, crowded along the entirety of the far living room wall, are tombs of the histories and archaeologies of different countries and continents on oak backless shelves. There are cultural trinkets to match. Brass and ivory. Everything looks aged and worn. Off center from the books hangs a Russian icon of Jesus with light radiating around his head. It is cracked down the middle, as if the canvas had been torn in half and secured back together, ever so imperfectly, so the sides of his face are misaligned.

Through the large windows reserving the rest of the wall space, I can see the snow flurry in differing directions. It causes the brown leaves on the tree to tremble. I wondered if she ever looked at these books or if they were just there so she would feel the facade of intellectual worldliness when she came home. A Time magazine lies on the end table, dated May 08, and is open to a story, "How Wall Street Sold Out the World," decorated with a picture of a man headfirst in a black hole. Only his feet remain undevoured.

Her phone rings, and I let the machine answer. The blinking light patiently announces five unchecked messages. Her voice picks up, informing she will be at the doctors for an hour and will be back at three. It is my aunt calling out of lonely obsession to ensure I keep the plants alive. Most of the flowers in the house are fake. The only authentic ones are in the adjoining dining room on the table. My aunt had been diligently coming over every weekend for the past six months to care for them.

I rush into her bedroom with the sudden compulsion to unpack. I had always craved the adventurous newness of things. Now I yearned for stability. In order to organize my effects, I have to empty the closet of hers. It is overflowing with robes and flowery silk blouses with Easter egg colors, placed in order of clothing type. I tear open the packages of the few selected belongings I shipped here weeks ago and dump their contents on the floor. I disrobe her hangers, paying close attention everything is folded neatly into the just-emptied boxes. I take the shoes out of their places in the rack and exchange them with mine. The closet is now filled with stylized black and red suits and stiletto pumps. I leave everything else as is, except the icon of Jesus, which I store face down in one of the boxes of her clothes that I place in the guest bedroom.

I lie down on my back in the middle of the hall that connects every room. There has to be at least two clocks in each room. From the hall floor, I can hear all of their intertwined metronomes. I contemplate taking their batteries out, unable to decide if the sound is meditative or nerve-racking. For now, I resolve to cover up the noise. I left my sound system in Charlotte, along with most of my other belongings. On my most recent trip to Mexico, my iPod was stolen, along with all the jewelry I owned, including those from long-ago trips to Paris, Turkey, and London and many my grandmother had given me over the years. It is easier to start over when you no longer have as much to lose. Searching the house, I cannot find any means of playing music. There is no stereo or Internet. In her bedroom, I find an old alarm clock with a manually adjustable radio. Changing the station from classical, I cannot readily get another to come in clearly. Finally when I find something I recognize, I stop.

SAVE EVERYTHING

DAVE ONOFRYCHUK

I let in a dumb goal last night. My crap team lost another game. I lie in bed and stare out the window at the grey sky and wish I had the curtains closed, cut the light in here. It's just past noon, and I still want to sleep. My mom, upstairs in her own bed, probably has her curtains closed. She's been coming home for lunch, staying in bed the rest of the day, depressed. Her boss understands, but she'll get herself fired. We're in a long stretch of limp and useless days, the two of us.

I roll over and call Kyle, the first-line centre for the University of Michigan. He packed his bags and left me here in the wasteland of college hockey north of the border—the Leftover League. He gets enough American scholarship money to run a small nation, and he says I shouldn't call it that. And I was better than him when we were kids. More control in my shot. Then one night at the outdoor rink, we watched this goalie. The pucks popped right off him like nothing. "Done," he kept saying. The whir of black rubber. The pop of his pads. Done. Done. He had broken down time into little events, and he owned each one. I watched him, transfixed. Shooting the puck isn't like that—so much left to chaos and chance.

The day Kyle was drafted, we threw rocks at seagulls from the boat launch across the lake from his parents' cabin, away from the pressure of his family. "Did you get called?" they kept asking. "Was there a call?" At the boat launch, he hung up his cell phone. "Number 198," he said. "Boston Bruins." That's all he said, as if it were happening to a stranger, but I could tell he was relieved. Just twelve picks from the end of the draft.

We turned twenty-one over the summer, him then me. He took me out. I drank three pitchers, shouted at pretty girls and cops. Those candles on the cake spelled one thing: TOO OLD FOR THE DRAFT NOW, YOU POOR BASTARD. Throwing rocks at birds that afternoon, I had secretly—foolishly—hoped for my own call. I'll be number 210. I'll be the last kid picked for teams at recess. Again. Just pick me.

Kyle's voicemail kicks in. I hang up and cover my face with an arm, and I'm on the ice again. The opposition comes in on the rush, the winger rips a shot on the fly, the puck comes off my blocker— done—and everyone's off in the other direction. Reflexes take over. Instincts set in. The new me emerges, strong and confident. No pill can match it.

And Martha Johnson comes to games. Something about a hockey game and so many hot girls. "Best cheap hockey in town," she told me in our Intro to Lit class last semester. She scribbled her number on the corner of a notebook page—we'd partner up for the midterm project, figure out schedules. But I had road games, too many road games. People hated group work with me. I was never around, and my work was half-assed, finished as the guys cheered on Pulp Fiction or Fight Club on the bus TVs. Save yourself, I told her. And she did, closed her notebook on her half-written number.

We're going to finish under .500 again. Miss the playoffs. Again. I can feel it. Go, Golden Bears.

I rest my head on the edge of the mattress and stare at the shirt crumpled on the floor, my Oilers shirt with Hollander's number on the back. A goalie too.

The phone rings. Kyle says, "You called."

"I let in a dumb goal last night."

"No one saves everything."

"I let it in, and we lost."

"But not in the last five games. The Internet says five. I thought you'd never call again. Five in a row—our goalie can't do that."

"No one wants a small goalie."

"How about the pills?" he asks. He always asks.

"They keep me up all night."

"Stuff for sleeping?"

"Too groggy the next day."

"The anxiety?" His code word for mania. Last year, we came to the house and walked in on my mom dancing on the coffee table in high heels and a gold bikini. She had cooked her transmission, no money to fix it. Then a Christmas bonus. No bonuses her whole life and then: a bonus. The volume on the stereo was turned up as far as it would go. At her brother's wedding that summer, she peed in the bushes outside the church after the ceremony. My dad couldn't hack this kind of thing; he's been out of the picture a very long time. I've felt it, not so off the cliff, but still. It's hard to explain. If joy is fire, mania is lava.

"Hello?" Kyle says.

"I'm here."

"You're staying level, then?" It always goes like this. We'll both graduate in the spring, and he'll have his shot at the NHL—the closest I'll ever get to training camp, and he shuts me out. Doesn't let me ask questions.

"I'm not on anything," I say. "My focus goes too out the window." I feel my voice press hard in my throat. He'll get cut from camp, and soon—we both know this. His numbers are way down after one amazing season at Michigan, one fluke season. But they'll find him room on a feeder team in the minors, give him a longer tryout next year.

"I graduate, then what?" I ask. I always ask. "Men's league. Skate around with the discard pile." I'm too small for anything else. We both know this too. A scout has said this about me; it's official. Only a few more games now where the shots are counted, a save percentage calculated, scores printed in the paper. It's everything, and I can't save it.

A sigh, a long sigh from Michigan. "Best undrafted goalie in Alberta," he says and hangs up. I doze on and off until the phone in the living room rings and voicemail takes the call. It rings its cycle again and stops for the voicemail. It rings again. Footsteps down the stairs, my mom's voice. Talking and talking. She busts in without knocking.

"Mom! Seriously! I could be masturbating."

"You have to take this. Take it. Take it." She shoves the phone in my face. Our assistant coach, a man on edge, a real screamer. Like a phone call in a bad late-night movie version of my life, he says, "Hollander's sick—a freak thing. They need a backup tonight. You in?" He sounds really annoyed.

"Sick?"

"You want it—yes or no?"

"What about their guy in Oklahoma?"

"No time to fly him up. Listen."

"They want me?"

"No one owns you, and you're hot right now."

"We lost last night."

"Oh my God," he says. "Yes or no?" He's so put out he's practically shouting. My mom walks out of the room and throws her arms in the air and does a dance like she's scored a Super Bowl touchdown. Uh-oh. "It's just one game," he says. "Ninety-nine percent, you won't even play. Ninety-nine point nine. They'll call this guy in Calgary—"

"No, no, no. No. I'll do it. Pick me. Yes."

"You're backing up Filipa tonight. Game's at seven thirty. Show up at four or five, I don't care. Was that your mom? I had to repeat myself—I thought she was deaf." The man does not like to repeat himself. "She crazy or what?"

"Four or five, okay," I say and hang up.

And whoa. The Edmonton Oilers. My mom is singing wildly in the kitchen, not even words, just nonsense sounds. Pots and pans smash down hard on the kitchen linoleum. I don't even want to know what she's doing. This new medication isn't working for her. I jump out of bed and throw on some jeans and the Hollander shirt for good luck, then take it off, put on another. He's sick—bad luck. I grab my keys and drive away.

Three hours to kill. I park in a small lot by the river and climb a stairway up the valley. The clouds are low today. The city is misty and smudged up and sad. The North Saskatchewan, half frozen, sits motionless under the cars streaming over it. Beyond the valley, the white HOTEL sign at the West Edmonton Mall shines like a beacon, tiny in the distance. When we were kids, Kyle and I played a game in the parking lot, when it was the biggest mall in the world: Who could spot the license plate from the farthest place? Who would find Florida or Texas today? Only for a while, Texas didn't count. The Dallas Stars kept beating the Oilers in the playoffs—if we ignored Texas, it would go away.

It gets hard to remember that the Oilers were so good for a while. Five Cups, seven seasons. The magical eighties—and it's all just the dim blur of my first memories. I was gypped. My team was a dynasty, and I had no idea.

I take Fox Drive to the university. The cranes move slowly over steel frames and campus rooftops, everywhere it seems. I count six, all with their Christmas lights gleaming out of season. They stand there like guardians; it's a peaceful sight. Pedestrians on Whyte Ave put their heads down in the icy wind, pull their jackets tighter around themselves. The bars will be full tonight, Friday night, the game playing high in the corners on cheap TVs. A tinge of excitement drops to my stomach like a brick of dread.

I drive to the Edmonton Ski Club and walk out to the top of the hill. The chairlift stands empty, unmoving. It's been crap for snow this year. Across the valley, the skyscrapers downtown feel close enough to touch. The clouds move slowly overhead, reflected in the purple glass of Canada Place, where my grandpa took me for rides in the glass elevator in its hollow centre, before his heart quit. He watched every game on a small TV, hidden away in the basement behind stacked boxes in storage, like a satisfied hermit. He'd go crazy if he knew I was on the roster tonight. Crazier than my mom, even. I laugh at that and feel bad.

I'll call Kyle. I should call him. He'd love this. Then I snap my phone shut, put it back in my pocket. I get it now, why he doesn't say anything. I can't think of a way to explain this without feeling like I'm rubbing it in his face.

The afternoon curls away under my tires. I shut the car off outside the stadium zone for resident parking. I heave my hockey bag out of the trunk and catch the feeling of my first walk to the stadium, holding my dad's hand, watching fans in Oilers jerseys stream by us under street lights, asking him again and again about our seats. Were they good? Are you sure? How close? How close will we get?

At Wayne Gretzky Drive, I set the bag down at the light and watch the cars breeze by Rexall Place, big and looming, a twenty-sided concrete puck. I just want to be in the net. Filipa's down. I don't have to worry about it anymore. I've stopped the first shot—done. Everything's simple: the puck comes at me, I get in the way. Reflexes take over. Instincts set in.

I trek across the parking lot and stop. I should've parked here.

They would've validated it. Stupid. Stupid autopilot. I set the bag down and rub my sore shoulder. Who would walk six blocks with a bag full of pads? Idiot. Stupid. Why would they call me? My stomach floods with a prickly gush. I look down at my too-small hands and knead my thumbs into the palms. They won't stop shaking. What am I doing? Stop shaking already. What am I doing? What am I doing? What am I doing? What am I doing? This was a mistake. A mistake. This was a mistake. Stop shaking. I should turn back. Go home. Forget about it. No. Bad. Bad, bad, bad, bad, bad. I'm doing this. I'm doing it. Stop shaking.

I peer through the glass of the locked doors. A woman at the ticket booth looks up from her computer screen. I can't hear what she's saying. She's not getting up. I knock harder. I don't stop, not even looking at her anymore, staring at the grain elevators behind the lot, avoiding the gaze of the Gretzky statue holding high the Cup. She stops short of the doors and looks at me over the tops of her glasses.

"I'm on the team tonight?" I say. I don't mean it as a question. "Derek Chivers? That's my name?"

She doesn't say anything.

"Where should I . . . Is there someone you can call?" She disappears.

A grey-haired man in a dark suit welcomes me inside. He takes me to an office deep inside the building where I sign a one-day amateur tryout contract. "You won't get paid," he says. I nod. The contract's clear about that. He hands me the Oilers cap I'll wear on the bench and an envelope with five twenties in it. "For gas and parking. Keep the hat," he says. "The jersey's yours too."

He leaves and comes back with a copy of the contract, warm, right out of the machine, for my records. I hold the sheet as lightly as I can to keep from putting any creases in it. This is going in a frame on my wall.

We go through more halls to the locker room in the basement where he shows me the empty stall with my jersey hanging in it. He snaps his fingers in a fidgety way and leaves. I don't know who's more nervous about this, me or him. I pinch the jersey, rub the fabric between my fingers. My heart pounds an OhmyGod-OhmyGod-OhmyGod rhythm. Then I feel it, slushing down my head, melted candy to my veins. Oh no. My neurons are chanting, Off the cliff! Off the cliff! Quick, before I do something. Quick. It's bad. What do I do? Before I do something. Quick. Do something. What do I do?

I stick my head in the showers, the knob full blast on cold. My head freezes, burns, screams. It's all I can think about. The panic dissolves. It's over, almost over—everything not so sharp anymore. I turn off the shower, soaked to the waist, shivering.

Steve Roskin, the team's big free-agent catch in the offseason, turns from his stall, looks at me. The hardest, most accurate slapshot in the league. Just stares at me, not sure what to say. Goalies are weird—we have to be to want to face a puck at a hundred miles an hour. He's not sure if this is just part of my weird goalie deal or what. I can see it in his face. What should he say? Maybe he says something, breaks my pregame ritual, causes a problem. Finally, he says, "You're wet."

I say, "I am not." He just stares at me. I suck at jokes. I'm such a piece of garbage. We're so finished if I play. He throws me a folded towel. "Thanks," I say. I sit at my bench, holding my contract in wide-open hands, and I imagine a guy in a black ski mask raiding the place when the game's on. He can have my wallet, ID, whatever, but the contract—I couldn't ask for another copy. The man in the suit would be so busy, with a disaster like that, I'd never see it again. Stop. Stop it already. They have security. This is the NHL. This is the NHL. Or if there was a fire. Oh. Fire.

I have this sheet of paper in my hands right now—but in two hours, or three, or four? Stupid. Stop it. I put the contract carefully onto the top shelf and take my pads out of the bag, and I see that guy in the ski mask again. I see fire. I feel panic. The hat, the jersey, I can buy them. The contract's the only authentic thing, the only thing that proves it happened. I fold it into quarters—I make sure no one is watching—and wrap it in the long plastic-paper gas pump receipt from my wallet and slip the whole thing between my underwear and my hip. There. Safe from robbers and fire, my own sweat. There.

I put on my gear. The room fills with Oilers, these giant guys. They're all in a good mood. They've been unstoppable. Filipa's been the difference—the trade deadline grab that's made the GM look like a genius. The other backup was crap, and now Hollander's playing backup to this guy. He's forty, playing out of his mind, the best in his life. Best numbers in the league since All Star break. He comes into the room, he's walking on clouds. He literally bounces as he walks. The man glows. He says anything close to funny, all the guys laugh. He gets dressed and sits beside me on the bench and says, "Five in a row. Gooo, backups!" I'm not sure if he's talking about me or him or what; I just kind of nod. He puts out a fist. I bring a fist up. We touch knuckles. His hands are easily twice as big as mine.

We go to the ice for warm-up. Filipa and I set up shop at either end. The players skate in slow, easy strides and pound the puck like it's nothing. Stick goes down, puck goes away, back of the net. I don't even feel it whiz by. Another one, then another. Another. A voice in the back of my head shouts, Wake up! Then: to the left, top shelf—done. Right, down low—done. Five hole—done. Five hole—done. I'm not even thinking about it now, just saving.

Then I see it in them, like their brains are all connected: his glove is weak. Glove-side! I can't even get a piece of the puck. Glove-side! Glove-side! Glove-side! The pucks are pouring in now. They're robots, accuracy like that. Glove-side! Glove-side! What am I doing? What am I doing? What am I doing? What am I doing? What am I doing? What am I doing? What am I doing? What am I doing? My butthole puckers up so hard it hurts.

Then the voice: Just get in the way! I scoot way over to the right to save a shot with my shoulder. I whip my blocker left over the open net—done. My blocker is lightning. It's that fast.

We leave the ice for the Zamboni. The coach says a few things, focus points for the game. An interim coach, this guy, a former assistant—the head coach couldn't cut it before All Star break. I keep forgetting this guy's name. I've read it in the paper. We line up in the hall under the bleachers. The house lights go off. I watch the silhouettes of the guys ahead of me, swaying side to side, tapping their sticks on their skates and the floor. The announcer calls over the speakers: "Your . . . Edmonton . . . Oilerrrrs!" The crowd goes ballistic. The bleachers above us go ca-crunch, ca-crunch. The line moves forward. Players push off onto the ice under the replica oil derrick that spurts out white fireworks. I'm shaking again. My heart is about to explode. The crowd goes nuts. Music blasts over us. The derrick's hoisted up behind me as I shuffle out. The Oilers logo dances around the ice from an overhead light on a swivel. Purple and green lights flash all around us. The Oilers and visiting New York Islanders skate in speeding circles on each half of the rink. I slide to a stop. What am I doing here? I'm going to cry. Roskin comes by, gives me a curt nod, taps his stick on my leg pads, and says, "Skate."

The announcer calls out the roster. I skate to the bench, and the guys line up along the boards in front of me; we bow our heads for the anthems, and the first period starts. It's back and forth for the first ten minutes. I freeze up every time Filipa goes down—like he's turned to glass. Get up! Get up! Roskin winds up from the point on a power play and slaps the puck in. One–nothing, us. The period ends. We head to the lockers. Guys change jerseys, readjust pads, put on new tape while some see the trainers. The coach says a few more things about the game.

Second period. I'm scared I'll throw up. I have not calmed down. We'll score again, and everyone on the bench will go nuts, and that'll be me on the end there, the guy blowing chunks. The plastic receipt in my underwear is slick and itchy. Idiot. Stupid. Someone knocks on the glass around the bench, right behind me. There's no way I'll turn around and let the fans see how scared I am. A woman says something loudly, and I turn. It's Martha, in a tight black sweater and dark jeans, dressed up for a night out. I've never seen her look this good. She's standing on the bleacher steps, bent over two guys in their seats.

"What're you doing here?" I ask.

"What am I doing here?" she says.

"They called me."

"No shit," she says.

One of the guys pushes her, says, "Hey, go away."

I need her number. She wouldn't say no to an Edmonton freaking Oiler. What do I say? How do I ask? What do I do? Where do I write it? She steps back and waves at me. "I'll find you on Facebook," she says and walks up the bleachers. Her ass looks great in those jeans.

I look back to Filipa. His secret, I know it. I scan the crowd in the lower bowl for a hot brunette sitting alone—no, with friends. She'd be awesome, have lots of friends. She's here somewhere.

Martha Johnson is in the crowd. I smile and the muscles in my face go: What is this strange thing we're doing? Filipa crouches in net as the Islanders come at him on the rush. A meteorite—I want a meteorite, just a tiny one, to shred through the roof and knock him down. Everything cools right down inside me. Please, God, please. Let me play.

The buzzer sounds for the second intermission. I open the gate again for the guys coming off the ice, and we file down the hall to the dressing room. A man in a brown suit says to me, "We've heard your story. We want to do an interview after the commercials." He puts a microphone in my face. Roskin looks from me to the man and says, "Hey, I'll do it if you want."

"I got it," I say. Anxiety gone. I'm an exhausted, squished-up shell. Finally. Hopefully, it'll last an hour, till the game ends. Roskin starts down the hall. I say, "You know, I kind of wish I was with the other guys. I want a chance at that slapshot."

He doesn't look back, but I can tell he's smiling. "I like my chances with the guy they have now."

The interview's a blur.

We win. I don't play a single minute. But it becomes my mom's favourite story: watching me play for the Oilers. My first three games after that, I post consecutive shutouts for the Golden Bears. The Gateway calls. "Did you know," the reporter says to me, "you're in the hunt for the CWUAA record for most consecutive scoreless minutes?" On the front page, they run a picture of me sitting on the bench for the Oilers, hunched over, my hands between my knees. If you look close enough, you can tell I want to hurl. The headline reads: "One-time Oilers Backup Seeks League Record." There are stacks and stacks of it in the newspaper racks of the Student's Union Building.

Before our next game, I wake up for a three-a.m. piss and stare into the bathroom mirror. With the other guys? I said that? To the star player? On the best team since All Star break? The guys on the other team? I had opened my mouth and said that? To his face? Just show me a hole, give me a cave.

They score on the first rush, twenty seconds into it. They win 7–2. I'm pulled after a four-goal first period. They win the next game, 5–1. Coach pulls me after three goals in five minutes. The game after that, I face fifty shots, three more than the other guy, in an 8–7 win. I shake my head at a game like that. Uh, defense? Anyone? Embarrassing. It's news for all the wrong reasons. I had a 0.86 save percentage. Total garbage. A game like that, it was like watching two drunks pound each other's faces in. But we won. Before that game, I stared for five minutes at that contract, now in a frame on my wall, its fold marks smoothed over with the iron I borrowed from Martha.

SKIN AND BONES

MATT DOOGAN

Dusk was deepening when Robert saw the cat, creeping into his backyard through a hole in the fence. It was a scrawny little thing, with grey fur and greenish-yellow eyes that glowed as it approached. The fire burning in the pit provided a small amount of light, but Robert was seated at the edge of it, shrouded in shadow, wrapped in a heavy dark coat to keep out the bite of the cold—the fire only warmed one side, after all. He wasn't sure if the cat didn't notice him as it walked toward the fire or if it was just too cold and hungry to care.

Still, as the cat walked into the light of the fire, Robert could see that the cat was in better condition than he'd originally thought. It was skinny, to be sure—this was no pampered housecat, he could see its ribs through its fur—but its eyes were clear and alert, and it moved with a quiet grace. Why had he thought it had looked haggard when he first spotted it?

"Hey, cat," he said quietly. "Come to share my fire?"

He'd half-expected the cat to turn around and bolt at the sound of his voice, but instead, it turned and looked at him, head cocked slightly to one side. It wore no collar; maybe it was a stray, or maybe a feral cat from deep in the woods that bordered his small neighborhood. Probably not feral, he reflected, if it was willing to get so close to a human. What was its story, then? He doubted it was from his neighborhood; he didn't talk to his neighbors, but he would have seen or heard them out looking for it if they'd lost a pet. It must have come from farther away.

The cat stared at him for several seconds, whiskers twitching, and then sat down close to the fire. It looked into the flames for a moment, then laid down, paws tucked underneath its body so that it could spring up at a moment's notice.

"Just make yourself at home, why don't you?" Robert said. "Well, you aren't going in my house. You can't let just anyone into your home, you know. Too many out there will take advantage of that. Bad things can happen." The words sounded bitter to his ears.

The cat offered no opinion of its own. It made no sound as it laid by the fire. It hadn't made a sound since it had arrived. Robert appreciated that.

He stared at the cat for a long moment, considering what he should do with it. There might be a family somewhere out there still looking for it. An image came unbidden to his mind of a little girl with tears in her eyes as she forlornly called out for her beloved pet. His chest felt tight, and he banished the thought as quickly as it had come. It hit too close to home.

So what was he to do, then? He could let it enjoy the warmth of the fire, but he couldn't help feeling like he should do more. Did he have anything he could feed it? He didn't have much food in the house; he needed to go to the store. But maybe he had some milk he could give it.

"What do you think, cat?" he said. "Would you like some milk? I can do that much for you, at least."

He stood up, slowly, wincing against the pain in his hip and shoulder. They'd been aching for weeks now, and the cold weather had only made things worse. Old bones, he thought to himself as he walked to his back door. The cat's eyes followed him, unblinking, as he went.

His house was as he remembered it—cold, dark, and empty. He turned on a light in the living room and made his way toward the kitchen. On the way, he passed by a table by the wall with a framed photograph on it. He, his wife, and their two young daughters. He and his wife were smiling, and the girls had been captured in open-mouthed shrieks of laughter. He barely gave it a glance.

A pile of mail covered most of his kitchen table, with only a small space cleared for him to eat. The mail was mostly sympathy cards, dating back months, but an envelope from his lawyer sat unopened on top of the pile. His updated will. He needed to review it and go in to meet with the lawyer tomorrow.

He opened the door to his refrigerator, finding it nearly empty. No milk. He sighed. Maybe downstairs?

Robert unlocked the door to the basement and flicked on the light, revealing a flight of wooden stairs. They creaked as he descended into a basement that was a large main room almost the size of the house's footprint with a small bathroom near the stairs. Grey, dingy concrete walls framed the space, and the floor was a single concrete slab. A large stack of cardboard boxes took up the western third of the room, but it was otherwise empty save for the refrigerator in one corner, the workbench with assorted tools along one wall, and the man chained in the corner farthest from the stairs.

He was huddled in a ball, naked except for a dirty pair of shorts. His face and body were covered in bruises and dried blood, and a mass of burn scars crisscrossed his chest and his back. He was a bit younger than Robert, though he looked much older now. He didn't have much hair left on his head. He'd been average sized when Robert had first met him, but now he was nearly emaciated, ribs visible through his scarred and battered skin.

Robert crossed over to stand in front of him and inspected the man's chains, though it was just habit at this point. He was long past the point of trying to escape. Finding the chains secure, Robert straightened up, meeting the man's eyes as he looked up at him. He saw fear there, terror, but also mixed in was a look that was almost— pleading.

"Please," the man croaked. "Please let me go. I'm begging you."

"Do you like cats, Hunter?" Robert said as he walked over to the refrigerator, his tone casual. "I never cared much for them myself. Always saw them as just another mouth to feed, not really good for much of anything unless you had a mouse problem. But now, I wonder if I was wrong. They have a kind of nobility to them. At least, some of them do."

"Please . . . Please," Hunter croaked through lips caked and dry. "I can't take any more." His eyes, wild with fear, were fixed on the acetylene torch on the workbench next to the refrigerator. "Please."

Robert wasn't reaching for the torch, though. Instead, he opened the refrigerator door and pulled out a carton of milk. There wasn't much left, and it was a couple of days past the expiration date, but when he opened the carton and sniffed at it, it smelled fine. He'd had some in his coffee when he was in the basement just that morning, so he felt okay about giving it to the cat. "Cats were considered sacred in ancient Egypt, you know," he said. Then he paused for a moment, a slight frown appearing on his face. "At least, I think they were. That's one of those things you just hear, but I never bothered to check if it was actually true. I should do that sometime," he added, almost absently.

As he walked back to the stairs, milk carton in hand, Hunter's voice called out behind him, louder now, but still weak. "Please." he said. "Look, I . . . I know you won't let me go. So, please, just kill me."

Robert stopped at the bottom of the stairs and spoke without turning around. "Forty days," he said, his tone tight and controlled. "I told you it would take you forty days to die for what you did. This is only day twenty-three."

A despairing moan rose behind him as Robert ascended the stairs, but he paid it no mind. When he reached the top, he turned off the light, plunging the basement into darkness once more, and locked the door behind him. He went into the kitchen to retrieve a saucer for the milk, but as he took it out of the cabinet, he found his hands were shaking so badly he almost dropped it. Taking a deep breath, he carefully set the saucer down on the counter and poured the last of the milk into it.

When his hands were steady again, he picked up the saucer and headed for the back door. He passed the photo of his family again, but this time, he stopped and stared at it for a long moment. He fixed on his wife's eyes, trying to see into their depths.

Finally, he turned away. He carried the saucer outside and set it down about halfway between his chair and the cat. The fire was burning low now, and the chill of the night air settled over him as he sat back down. "There you go, cat," he said. "It's yours if you want it."

The cat eyed the saucer warily, but Robert could see its whiskers moving as it sniffed the air. Finally, it rose and walked over to the saucer, where it stared at him for a moment before it began to lap up the milk. It drank until the saucer was empty, then walked back over to the fire. It didn't lay back down, though. Instead, it sat, staring at him, and gave a hoarse little meow.

Robert watched the cat as the fire burned low. Finally, he stood and walked over to his back door. He opened it and held it open, standing to one side of the door, and looked back over at the cat.

"I don't think you have a place to go," he said. "You can stay here for a while if you want. You don't seem a bad sort, and the . . . unpleasantness will be over soon. I can't promise I'll be as good as your last family, but I'll feed you and keep you warm. And . . . maybe you'll make the place feel a little less empty."

His hand was starting to shake again, and he gripped the doorknob tightly. "I have to go visit the lawyer tomorrow, but maybe I can put that off for a while if you move in." He looked at the yellow-green eyes staring back at him from the dark. "So, what do you say, cat?"

The cat tilted its head at him, then turned and ran off into the darkness, back the way it had come.

Robert stared after it silently, his jaw clenched. His gaze flicked down to the now empty saucer by the fire pit, but he made no move to pick it up. He simply stood there, his hand still clutching the doorknob, staring off into the darkness where the cat had run. Why had it fled? What had driven it away?

But he had no answers, so he went inside and closed the door behind him as the fire burned its last, leaving behind nothing but ash and dead wood.

THE RED DRESS

SKEETER WILSON

She walked into the bar, and I knew right away she was different. Beside her walked a French bulldog. Well, it looked like a French bulldog, but there may be more to that story. But it was not the bulldog that I noticed first. She was wearing a red dress, a hot number that was a little daring but not overstated. Yes, I noticed that red dress and the way it paid tribute to the woman who wore it, but that was not what I noticed first either. She was the perfect woman. It is hard to explain what that means exactly. What is the perfect woman, anyway? I had never had an answer for that. I suppose it may be because I had never seen a perfect woman before. It is that intangible confidence one feels that this is one with whom one could be a man. A man, in that soul sense that compliments a woman. Not any woman—this woman.

That is what I noticed first. But, I was not in the bar to find the perfect woman, and this one was too far above my pay grade. I don't mean she was uppity or anything like that. No, I could see she was real. It's just that just about anybody is above my pay grade. No, this is not some sort of self-loathing. I don't hate myself. I am pretty much okay with who I am. It's just that some people are born with a social gene that allows them to participate with the rest of society, and some people, like myself, are genetically incapable of interacting with humanity. That is where I come in, sitting at the bar, content to be by myself, preferring my own company rather than the awkward uncomfortableness of the company of others. I suppose that is why I am a writer—I get to talk about people, not to them.

She sat down next to me, but I was already lost in other thoughts, so I did not notice until I felt the warm licks on my elbow. I turned slightly and saw she was holding the Frenchie on her lap, and its head was dangling over her side licking my elbow.

"Hello buddy," I said, and I patted its head and was rewarded with more licks.

"Oh! I am sorry, is Winston bothering you?" she said, but made no move to pull her French bulldog away from me.

"Oh no," I said, "I am enjoying his affection. I get along with dogs better than people. Well, more honestly, I don't really get along with people, just dogs."

"I understand," she said. "We have that much in common already."

She really did look stunning in that red dress. I returned to my beer. I don't really know why I chose beer. I like beer well enough, but I prefer a well-constructed whiskey sour or a wine. Not just any wine, my tastes are not sophisticated enough for red, so I like a not-too-dry white. I think I order beer often because it is a big glass, and it gives me an excuse to sit for a long time lost in my imagination. So the beer is the prop for the theater of my mind.

"I will have a Riesling, not too dry," she said.

That sort of startled me. I was willing to forget that the perfect woman was sitting next to me. I had even passed up the opportunity to explore why she mentioned that we had something in common. But I had set up a sort of absent-minded routine with Winston where in return for his incessant licking, I gently scratched behind his ear.

"Well, I suppose that makes two things we have in common," I said.

The perfect woman gave me a look. It is a little difficult to explain the look. On the outset, it seemed the message of the look was one of annoyance. Not too much annoyance, not anger really, but a sort of annoyance that did not really mean back off—at least not completely. I knew I would puzzle over that look for a long time. It was a message with a slight building of dark clouds. Enough dark clouds to pay attention to, but on the other hand, it was more like dark clouds that surround a beautiful sunset. The kind of dark clouds that one appreciates because they make the sunset more beautiful.

They give the sun's last glow boundaries, and the wisps of water-laden air refract the sun's light into a cascade of blending colors. The kind of dark clouds that one does not really want to go away. I realized then, that even disturbance on the face of the perfect woman was still perfection. I was in awe.

"I don't drink beer," she said.

"I can live with that," I said. "But when I drink wine, I only drink white wine, and then, only wine that is not too dry. I don't really enjoy red wine. I suppose that means my tastes are not sophisticated, but I can live with that too."

"Then I suppose we have that in common too," she said. "No sense in seeing what else we have in common, is there?"

"I suppose not," I agreed. And I did agree. It was the perfect conversation with the perfect woman. Anything else, I might have said, would only ruin that. I was content.

"My girlfriends have come," she said, not looking directly at me. "Enjoy your beer. Come on, Winston, let's go see them."

She placed Winston on the floor and briefly brushed some dog hairs from her red dress as she glanced toward me, and our eyes briefly met. She had no expression, but I could see amusement in the corners of her eyes.

"Enjoy yourself," I ventured. "And Winston, buddy, I hope we meet again."

With that, the perfect woman with the French bulldog named Winston walked to some corner of the room behind my back. I riveted my eyes on my glass of beer to keep from staring rudely after her, forcing my mind to the task of the moment—the task of nursing my beer in the comfort of myself. I chose to believe that the moments that followed were just like all the moments before the perfect woman with the red dress came in the door. Soon I heard laughter and affectionate voices calling for Winston and the hum of pleasant conversation. It had been a long time since I had looked at the corner of the room from where I now heard the laughter. I was not tempted to do so at that moment either. But it did feel slightly pleasant to know that there was a corner filled with voices and laughter, that the silence of me with my beer at the corner stool was not so silent, and I could welcome the difference.

Stories about a perfect woman, especially one who wears a red dress, with whom there was an exchange of a pleasant conversation, should rightfully end at this point. Some epiphany, some change in the protagonist to make a complete story, some subtle moral lesson learned. Instead, during my silent contemplation of how the moment should end, I felt a warm licking on my leg.

"Winston, buddy, what are you doing over here in the cheap seats?" I stepped off the stool briefly and picked Winston up. I started to turn toward the corner where the laughter continued uninterrupted and then thought better of it and sat back down on the stool. Winston turned over and hung his head off to the side of my lap like I had seen him do with the perfect woman. I began to lightly rub his belly. I could feel his body relax into my lap with each stroke, and he licked his lips in gentle contentment. I turned halfway around in the stool so that if the world's most perfect woman looked for Winston she could easily spot him on my lap.

I began to contemplate the alternatives of what would happen next. It seemed plausible that Winston would soon grow tired of his belly rub and once again seek the company of the perfect woman in the red dress. Certainly, if I were Winston, that would be my choice—there could be no real contest about which lap I would prefer to be laying across. But then I chose not to allow my imagination to wander too much further. Or the second alternative would be that the perfect woman in the red dress would come and reclaim her right of companionship with Winston. I certainly did not begrudge her that right, but I had no clever plan as to what cogent phrase I might concoct that would encourage a slight smile or, better still, that intriguing look of annoyance.

I tried for a moment to come up with a word beside *perfect* to describe her. After all, I am somewhat of a wordsmith, and coming up with alternative words is my business, but then I realized that this was foolishness. I was thinking far too much about the woman in the red dress, and soon she would come get her dog. I would oblige and return to the same glass of beer that I now was unable to reach because I was occupied with holding and rubbing the belly of Winston. But like I said, the beer was only a prop anyway.

It is hard for me to decide, at times, if I am an exceptionally observant person or one who is hopelessly unaware of his surroundings. I know these seems like incompatible extremes, but at times, I match both. I can instantly pick up on a raised eyebrow, a finger twitch, a tell-tale glance, and I can spend a great deal of energy evaluating the flutter of a look, with surprising accuracy much of the time. But then, it seems, I completely miss details that are far more obvious.

I suppose that this is a painstakingly laborious way of mentioning that, while rubbing the belly of Winston and pining occasionally for a small sip of my beer, I noticed a tall latte cup sitting on the bar where the perfect woman in the red dress had been sitting. I had little doubt that the cup had not been there before the perfect woman showed up, and certainly no one else had ventured to my end of the bar. This was a sports bar, after all, and I always chose this corner precisely because it was the one spot in the bar where it was difficult to see a television. My corner belonged to the lonely or, as I prefer to define myself, the intriguing eccentric.

The perfect lady was certainly intriguing with her choice to sit at the quiet end of the bar. Interesting, but I did not have the sense that she was eccentric, probably just not a sports fan. I don't suppose being an intriguing eccentric is a useful calling card for the perfect woman.

What occurred to me as I contemplated the latte cup was this: Could she have left it there on purpose? Sort of like the lady who drops her keys so that a gentleman will rush to pick them up and hand them to her while she blushes slightly and thanks him for his kindness? Was I a dope who had missed an obvious opportunity to reengage in conversation with the perfect woman?

It was not hard to remove that possibility from my mind. First, because I saw no indication that she wanted a further conversation. She seemed as happy as I was to let the whole conversation die the pleasant way that it had. However, it did intrigue me that I even entertained the possibility that she had left the cup there intentionally. I really did not want to pursue things a little more with the perfect woman in red, did I?

But why exactly was I holding Winston in my lap? Was I playing my own little game to cause a conversation to take place that I was not man enough to create on my own? Well, that could have been true; my initiatives at making conversations with women inevitably ended in train wrecks.

Then it occurred to me how long I had been holding Winston in my lap. By now, the perfect woman in red knew exactly where her companion was. Why was she content to leave her dog with me? Had she intentionally let him come to me in the first place, assuming I would bring him back to her? Had she left me the cup and then sent me the dog. Was she playing a game with me just like I was with her?

This, of course, was all an absurdity. The most obvious answer was the most likely. She left the cup because, either, she did not want it or she simply forgot it. She saw me holding Winston and decided that I must be enjoying doing so because I made no effort to bring him back to her. As long as I was content, she was going to enjoy her friends. Good for her, because I was enjoying holding Winston. Like I say, I don't really get along with people, just dogs.

I know, I know, there is too much internal dialogue in this story, and it is time to bring the perfect woman in red back into the scene. However, consider this: In a good story, there should be at least three things, a protagonist, a tension (sometimes in the form of an antagonist), and a change (in the perspective of the protagonist). This is my story, of course, and I am the one sitting at the bar, so my part of the internal dialogue is easy. Therefore, the only tension so far is my own internal tension at the appearance of the perfect woman in a red dress.

It is precisely the fact that I do not have insight into the internal dialogue of the perfect woman in red that my tension even exists. If I knew she was curious about me, my internal dialog would end as would the story. If I knew she was not interested, my tension would also be over, and the story would also end, though perhaps more melancholy. So when the moment occurs that I know for certain what she is thinking, there is no more story to tell.

I am in no hurry for this story to end. I sort of like the little things that keep me intrigued about the perfect woman. It turns the story into a sort of serial television show where the couple of interest never really kiss and everyone waits for the season finale, hoping for a resolution. But of course, if the series is to continue, the resolution must be both incomplete and unsatisfying, in order to bring the audience back the next season.

But this all assumes, that I am the protagonist of the story in which the tension that I am building around myself is the true tension of the story and that the change, whatever it is, will occur to me. Some writers are cleverer than that. Sometimes the main characters are not protagonists at all. Sometimes the actual tension is not introduced until later, or even until the end of the story. Though one cannot be too clever about this, because the longer one waits to introduce the real protagonist and the real tension to the reader, the more it feels like a cheap trick.

However, beside the perfect woman and myself, and Winston, I have indirectly introduced other characters without mentioning them. I have introduced a bartender, I have introduced a bar with sports fans watching television, and I have introduced the friends of the perfect woman. These are all fair game for important roles in this story. Anyone could become the protagonist, and anyone could introduce a new tension, as long as it is sooner rather than later.

"Sir, is this your coffee, or should I throw it out?" The voice of the bartender startled me a little. (See how easy introducing a new character is?) She was kind of cute, I suppose. I could tell she got plenty of tips, even from the men who were not drunk.

"It's not mine," I said. "It belongs to the same person that Winston here belongs to. Just move the cup next to my beer, and I will get it to her when she comes for my little friend."

"Oh! He is so cute!" With that, she leaned over the bar and stroked Winston on the belly a time or two. The bartender wore a low-cut blouse, which dragged slightly across the bar, making the source of her tips more evident.

Clearly a new tension has been introduced into this story, a whole new dynamic, a possible source of misunderstanding between me and the perfect lady in the red dress even before things had a chance to get started. But that is a cheap trick too, and the movie industry has worn it out.

"You have hardly touched your beer, sir," she said. She slowly slid back, making no effort to cover her assets. "Your drink is probably getting warm; would you like me to replace it with a cold one?"

"Oh, no thanks." I attempted a smile, riveting my eyes on a spot on her forehead, uttering silent curses on myself if I glanced down. "I lived in Europe long enough to enjoy a warm beer now and then."

That was a lie, of course. But the bartender was not wearing a red dress, and she was not the perfect woman. I made a mental note to not let this little fling affect my tip when I left. She smiled and moved to the next customer sitting a few seats down. The place was getting too crowded.

"Oh, I see you are using Winston to meet girls now?" The voice of the perfect woman was right behind me. I had already decided that this story was not going to turn on a misunderstanding between me and the perfect woman over the bartender, and here she was right behind me. Obviously, she had seen what I had seen. This could end ugly. I had not considered this in my options of how she would get Winston back.

"I suppose you saw all of that, then?" I heard myself saying. "I think she was looking for a bigger tip from me this time. Do you have a hundred dollars I can borrow?"

Well, Winston, buddy, this may be it for us.

Her quiet laugh calmed all fears I had that a new tension had been introduced into the story. She slipped back into the seat beside me and began to rub Winston's belly with me. Briefly our hands touched in the process. I caught myself seeking ways to continue the contact and then caught myself again and reached for the beer. "I suppose if you are going to do that for a moment, I should get a drink."

"If that is the same beer you have hardly touched it, or did you get another one?"

"No, ma'am, it is the same beer. I am having too much fun with Winston here to be drinking beer and chasing loose women."

She laughed and gave me a glimmer of that annoyed look again. I suppose I had not needed to reference the theatrics of the bartender again, but I suppose it was my relief that she understood the dynamic and that this story did not need to turn into another cheap movie trick. "Well, I thought you were enjoying Winston, so I decided to leave him with you until you had enough. Then I realized that you might have had enough a long time ago and were too modest to say anything. So, I decided to come rescue you from wicked women and see if you have had enough yet."

I chuckled slightly. "I am afraid that we have something else in common—we both overthink things. I will not begin to tell you all the things I have contemplated while holding our little buddy here. But the fact is that I am having one of the most pleasant evenings in a long time, and having Winston here to keep me company is a major part of that. Certainly, you can have him if you like, but if you are enjoying things as they are, I certainly am."

"Did I hear you say, 'our little buddy?'" she asked.

"Well, I think as long as Winston is in my bar, I can claim one percent emotional ownership. You still have majority shareholder privileges and can remove my share at any time."

"I am not certain I know what that means," she said. "But if you are okay with him, I will leave you boys alone. I think my girlfriends are ready to leave soon, and then I will come back and take over my responsibilities."

"Speaking of your responsibilities," I said, "is this your coffee?" I nodded toward the latte sitting next to my beer. "That bartender lady who wanted a big tip asked me if she should throw it away. I did not know your intentions, so I told her to leave it in case you still wanted it."

"Thanks for holding on to it. Yes, I still want it. It takes me awhile to drink my morning coffee."

"Morning coffee? You mean you have had that cup since this morning?"

"Don't go making fun of me too. I sort of have a reputation for taking all day to drink my morning coffee."

"So, let's review. You started with this cup this morning; you have been sipping on it all day. Since then you have had lunch and supper and drinks with your friends, and you still want to hang on to the coffee. Did I get that all right?"

"That about sums it up," she said.

"And you were mocking me for still having my first beer?" I said.

"I was not mocking you," she said. "I just was wondering if it was something else we might have in common."

"Okay, okay," I said. I hoped the roll in my eyes was convincing. "Let's not go finding out what all we have in common, okay?"

"Okay," she said, "it's a deal. If you don't mind hanging on to my coffee as well, I will pick it up when I pick up Winston."

"Sounds good. I will carefully watch the cup to make certain it does not go anywhere." She smiled slightly. The perfect woman and her red dress walked back to her friends and the laughter. I realized that I really did want to find out what else we might have in common. But then I mentally kicked myself for the thought. After all, I mused to myself, I get along with dogs, not people.

People like stories because they reflect life. The protagonist, the conflict, the change. Intuitively, we all understand that these are the basic elements of human existence. We exist, we struggle with our existence, and we come to new levels of understanding as a result. Most stories about relationships get the story exactly wrong. There is the one who wonders how the other person feels, then there is the conflict that puts the relationship in jeopardy, then they fall in love and live happily ever after.

But this cannot be. If the objective is love, and if this love is what begins the happily ever after, then there is no more story to tell. It ends when the relationship begins, and that could spell disaster for the relationship if there is no story to tell. The beginning of the relationship should be the beginning of the story, not the end.

This, I think, is the big difference between Eastern and Western ideas when it comes to relationships. In the West, people fall in love and get married. In the East people marry and spend the rest of the relationship falling in love. The latter is, statistically speaking, a healthier approach to a long story-filled life. This is not to say that I am in favor of arranged marriages, but I suppose I have lived in odd places long enough to feel a little suspicious about the value of the Western idea of romance. This is one of the reasons I am not good at relationships, I think about this sort of stuff too much. And I want a story that lasts forever, not one that ends before it begins.

"Still have that coffee?" she said, interrupting my internal dialogue and sitting back down beside me.

"You were not gone long; who did you miss most me or Winston?" I said, mentally kicking myself for not thinking before saying that.

"You seem like an interesting person," she said, evading the actual question. "My friends are going home now, so I decided to come back and get my things." She leaned in slightly against my shoulder as she began to stroke Winston's belly. I could feel her warm breath fluttering the edge of my beard.

Without thinking, I moved my arm and rested it on the back of her bar stool. I don't know why I did it exactly, but my shoulder seemed to be slightly in the way. I think it was an innocent move, but it is hard to say. My experience with women was such that the risk-reward ratio of putting my arm around a woman the first time I met her—or ever, for that matter—was not in my favor. Not even close.

It is hard for me to decide if I was really putting my arm around her or if I was just getting my arm out of the way so that she could pet Winston. She did not seem to be in a hurry to move him, and I certainly was in no hurry to end the moment. For a brief moment, she seemed to lean in just a little closer. I could feel her head resting ever so slightly more on my shoulder, and her arm rested on me as she stroked her French bulldog. Then she quickly sat up and leaned over and picked up her latte. She took a sip and turned to look at me as if she was about to say something and then thought the better of it.

"How exactly does a cold latte taste after this much time in a paper cup?" I asked. I think I was interested, but I was more interested in hearing her talk. Would I be able to pick up if she was annoyed with my arm which was still on the back of her chair? I felt a little caught. If I moved my arm, it might seem obvious that I had put it there intentionally; if I left it there I might look like I was assuming things not yet in evidence about *us*.

She gave me that charming annoyed look for an instant and then smiled. "It tastes good all day long. I don't like to throw it away but will finish it up before I go to bed tonight. I sort of had two glasses of wine tonight, and I really only need one to feel a little . . . well, this coffee will help."

"Well, Winston and I are in no hurry," I said. "Take your time working on that coffee. I certainly don't want you to drive home with two glasses of wine and all."

The perfect lady in the red dress smiled. She took a couple more sips and resumed her position on my shoulder with her arm draped across me, her hand rubbing Winston's belly. The Frenchie was clearly in heaven with all the attention. His half-opened eyes and occasional licking of his lips indicated utter contentment.

I do not know what got into me. But I realized that my hand was playing briefly with the perfect woman in a red dress's hair. And then it rested on the base of her neck. What am I doing? She did not move, and it seemed that I had no choice but to lightly massage the base of her neck. Why else was my hand there? Clearly, I had just ended the relationship long before the story had begun. No perfect woman in a red dress was going to put up with such nonsense. Her inevitable quick exit from my corner of the bar was going to come soon, I just knew it.

"Hmm, that feels nice," she said.

I swear that is exactly what the perfect woman in the red dress said to me. Fiction, it is said, must be more believable than nonfiction, and I can already hear the howls of protest from my critics that this is not a believable response from the perfect woman . . . especially to a lonely man sitting at the quiet end of the bar. But this is my story to tell, and this is how the perfect woman responded to me. There are times when the storyteller must ignore the critics.

I suppose if the movies and the claims of the straggle of friends I have encountered over the years were to be believed, this was the time to make my move. What a terrible expression that is. The truth is I sort of had made a move already. My hand was, after all, gently stroking the neck of the perfect woman, and she was not objecting.

But I am not a player. I suppose that could be one of the most obvious statements I have ever made. But it seems to me that a player is after just one thing, and I have always been after everything. So I have a habit of giving up opportunities and then mentally kicking myself for years afterward for being so idealistic. But this was the perfect woman in a red dress with a cool Frenchie named Winston, and I was definitely not going to be a player this time. This is my best explanation for the fact that when the perfect woman mentioned that it was time for her to go that I casually stopped stroking her neck and returned my hand to join hers in the task of stroking Winston's belly.

"Well, I have enjoyed getting to know Winston here. I suppose when you walk out that door, I will relinquish my one percent ownership for the time being. However, should you come back to this bar with friends and a cold cup of coffee, I will reclaim my right to excessive amounts of belly rubs for Winston while you enjoy your friends. Deal?"

"And what about the neck rub? Are you going to give me another one of those if I come back too?"

"As long as you admit we are friends, the neck rubs come as complementary," I said. "I noticed that you did not slap me when I did that. I was sort of expecting a slap or a quick exit."

She smiled. "I noticed that too," she said. "I don't know what got into me. Perhaps I should have just had one glass of wine. But yes, for that neck rub, I will admit to being friends. Neck-rub friends, I suppose. But you should know that tonight is unusual for me. I don't often come to bars with friends, and I usually don't drink two glasses of wine and let a stranger rub my neck."

"I am content with friends," I said. "I will take my chances on you coming back sometime." Yep, I am a killer player, alright. I successfully negotiated a just-friends relationship with the perfect woman in a red dress. But then, the truth was, I was not looking for the perfect woman before she walked in the door. That was why I was sitting at the quiet end of the bar in the first place.

She walked out just as she had walked in, the perfect woman in the red dress, pulling along her French bulldog. I had a brief encounter with the perfect woman, and I knew I was a better man because of it. And that is all it really takes to make this a complete story.

NILE

MATT MORSE

Take me to the river at night. Show me the black water. Show me the edge, where the bank crumbles and the water reaches up under the land and cuts it down. Make me stand on the edge, so my toes hang over into empty air. Tell me there are crocodiles down there. Describe the teeth and claws, the red eyes and the tails swishing, pushing them through the current, churning up the silt until the water is so thick with it even the fish can't see in that darkness.

Talk about the silt, about the way it will catch my feet, pull me down and wrap me up and fill my mouth and my nose and my eyes, soak into all the cracks and spaces of me until I'm more silt than anything, cold and dark, just like it.

Push me. Startle me. Grab my arm. Make me think I'm going to fall. Make me cry. Call me a baby. Pull me back from the edge. Tell me you won't push me in tonight but tomorrow you will. Or if not tomorrow then the next night. Or the next. Tell me it doesn't matter. Even if you never pushed me, the water would find me.

Tell me about the floods, about the rising water pushing up over the banks and snaking through the tall grass. Tell me it will cover everything, rise up and up and seep into our house, flow up the stairs and under the door and swallow me in my sleep. Tell me no matter where I go or how high I climb, the water will reach me and catch me and drag me down into the silt and the darkness full of red eyes and teeth and swishing tails.

Take me home. Tell me to shut up when we get to the door and I'm still crying. Punch me on the shoulder so I know you're serious. Wait for me to gulp down the sobs, until my breathing slows and evens out. Lead me up the stairs. Keep to the edges so they don't squeak. Don't speak, don't look at me as we sneak past mom's room and hear her breathing inside, slow and heavy.

Ignore me as we drop our coats on the floor and kick our shoes off in opposite corners of our room. Go to bed still in your clothes. Pull the covers over your head and block out the world while I change back into my pajamas and get in my own bed. Lie awake and stare into the darkness under your blankets. Feel like you're drowning, like the water and the silt are rising up around you, sucking you down into them.

Think about saying you're sorry. Want to. Almost do it. Open your mouth to say the words. Don't say anything. Don't know why you can't. Close your mouth and close your eyes and drown alone under the blanket.

MIST OF MEMORIES

CRAIG MILEY

The darkness grew heavier, sliding a thin sheet of pressure around the air that Amber passed through. She could feel the wolf's presence not far off and pushed herself to walk faster. It had started trailing them near the northern edge of Otter Lake, just as the sun was nearly set. At least that was when she thought she'd first caught sight of that ashen blur passing just along the edge of her vision, slipping between the shadows of the trunks, vanishing like a mirage when she turned to get a closer look.

As she carried her infant niece, Johanna, along the lake's western edge and wound down around to the southern tip, starting to curve back toward the parking lot and the old Ford, it slithered out from between a pair firs. The sun was now gone, the sky a pink hazy memory of its vanished warmth. In the waning light, she could make out the arc of the wolf's ribcage—tufts of matted fur clung tightly to it in some places, other places were bare and bald. It was alone.

The creature took a hesitant step forward. Amber reached for the bear mace Kyle had insisted upon when she had first suggested the idea of these weekly hikes. Her hands shook, and she fumbled with what the package had said was an easy-release safety. The orange cap came tumbling off and fell to the ground as the wolf took another step forward. Amber struggled to hold the can steady, trying to remember what her husband had said, the way his voice had come through the laptop's shitty speakers as Skype pulled a ventriloquist act and put them in the same room, she sitting on one side at Fort Richardson, Alaska, he on the other, in Kandahar.

"Do you really need to do this Amber?"

"I can't just sit at home anymore."

"Look, Amber, if this is about Samantha . . . your sister wouldn't—"

"Kyle . . ."

"I'm just trying to—"

"Don't. I'm doing this. Where is your bear spray?"

"Storage unit, the Action Packer tub on the second shelf. It should be right on top of my hiking gear."

"How do I use it?"

"Pull the safety. Aim for the eyes. Wait till it's in range, about thirty feet or so."

"Will I even have time left to spray if a grizzly is thirty feet from me?"

"If you stay calm."

"Thanks."

"I love you."

". . . I love you too."

"Remember . . . calm."

Staying calm was not amongst the things in Amber's head as the wolf began to limp closer, a gash on the outside of its left flank slowing its pace. She wasn't thinking anything. All that came were flashes of physicality: the weight of Johanna's head resting against her back as the baby slept in the brand new baby carrier, the sticky condensation of her sweat against the armpits of the old Bearpaw Festival t-shirt she was wearing under her new jacket, the whisper— no, the promise—of a breeze glazing across her face, tickling the tip of her nose, the burbling chatter of the lake's gentle ebb as a duck landed upon its glimmering surface.

The moment broke. The wolf surged forward through the night, and Amber's heart pumped so vigorously her vision jumped with every beat. She fumbled the bear mace, bumbling in her panic as she attempted to catch it, swatting it out of reach in the process. She hesitated. Her brain was so set on the bear mace as her only line of defense that she almost went for it anyways. Instinct won out.

Amber ran. The wolf chased.

Arms pumping furiously, chaffing against the thick, puffy straps of the baby carrier, she fled. The thick scrub of trees beside the lake reached out for her, pulling her onward with the enticing prospect of the open space between each trunk, yet turning her back at the same time; their staunch thicket of pliable branches jutting out in all directions. A formless wall of nature, she ran into it without hesitation, surrendering all sense of direction as the woods immersed her.

Johanna began to cry long wails of confusion. Amber's skin stung as the crisp September air seared through her light windbreaker. Aided by the multitude of tears made in the jacket as she collided with branches and plunged forward, the chill coursed beneath the cloth and under her skin.

Amber felt her niece's weight plunge downward with each step, causing the straps to dig ever deeper into her shoulders, putting more pressure on her knees. She felt it particularly in the left knee, which she'd thrown out as a junior in cross-country. The weight was relieved for the briefest of instants as her brand new Nike's pushed off the moist soil.

The shoes had earlier rubbed blisters on the ball of her right foot and on her left big toe as she hiked around the lake. The blisters ruptured now, sending a momentary sweep of fluid over her sweaty feet before the raw, red flesh beneath began to sear with each pounding stride. She never should have left without breaking the shoes in. It was what Samantha would have done. Amber could hear her trailblazing, mountain-climbing older sister's voice even now, whispering to her from the darkness, over the sound of her own ragged breaths and Johanna's cries.

"Didn't I teach you anything? You've got to wear them around the house, break 'em in first. I'll do the outdoors; you do the dresses. Trust me, and we'll be hiking up Flattop in a pair of matching dresses in no time."

The only time Amber remembered ever seeing her sister in a dress was at prom. Samantha had gone wearing a deep forest-green gown, arm in arm with the boy Timothy Shockey, who as a man twelve years later would father her only child after a one-night stand in a Montana motel. Amber couldn't recall what her sister had worn on her feet the night of prom. The thought slipped as one of Amber's laces caught on a root.

She collided with the unforgiving earth at full speed, skidding across the forest's undergrowth like a rock tossed over the thin surface of a lake. Soil filled her nostrils, and she spluttered for air. Her hands were bleeding. The red of her blood looked thick and black in the growing darkness.

The thought of the barely softened impacts of Johanna's head against the cushion as she'd hit the ground made Amber want to puke, but she didn't have the air. Coughing and gasping, she managed to stand, pushing herself on, certain the wolf was just behind her. The scent of fresh earth mixed with the taste of bile in her mouth as her senses reeled with the surge of adrenaline.

Amber's legs burned, and she'd begun to limp on her left leg, her knee sending an SOS out to her brain, crying out for a halt to the retreat. Her breaths were becoming harder and harder to pull in. It felt like her lungs had been perforated and torn into ribbons, unable to hold air. She could hear a soft fwump, fwump, fwump . . . fwump, fwump, fwump as the earth behind her was impacted by something large, something heavy. Johanna shrieked. Amber flung herself to the right, hopping to put just a little more distance between them and the wolf.

Without the lake's edge to guide her, she was irrevocably lost. The adrenaline had run its course, and Amber began to slow. Her long strides turned into wobbly stumbles—Oh, Kyle, you were right. This was stupid. I'm not her. I'm not her.

Johanna had finally run out of breath, and her cries became hiccups. I'm sorry, Sam. I'm sorry. A wall of fog lay ahead, stretching through the woods in both directions. Amber collapsed before it. Her limbs deadened, she slid a few feet farther, her face dragging along the ground, her bottom lip catching against root and earth. The taste of dirt filled her mouth as she let out a last gasp of surrender and her body came to a halt in the light, grey mist.

"I'm sorry, Sam." Her voice came out in a whimpering croak, clogged by the gritty soil. Samantha would never hear her. There was no one to listen now but the marble slab in a plot back in a Montana graveyard. No one to listen now but her sister's daughter.

"Get up. Come play." The sound of laughter bloomed in the air. Amber could suddenly smell her father's elderberry pie, familiar, welcoming. "Get up. Come play." A little girl stood a few feet past Amber. Her form was flickering and distorted, as if cast upon the mists by a projector. Even as a little girl, there was no mistaking

Samantha's shock of long, red hair and the familiar crook in the upper left corner of her lips. "Don't make me tell you again. Look, he's coming."

Samantha extended a small, delicate finger, pointing behind Amber. The wolf was plunging through the mist right toward them. Grimy fangs bared, saliva trailed along his jowls in thin streams.

"Come on."

"I can't," Amber said. Her swollen tongue clogged her speech.

"Let me help you." The little girl reached down and took her hand. Amber wrapped her scraped fingers around Samantha's smaller ones. Her sister's hand flickered and sputtered, but its firm grasp never waivered. Amber was yanked to her feet and tugged forward. She stumbled and nearly fell again. "Run!"

Amber took a step and then another. Samantha smiled and released Amber's hand, turning back the way Amber had come.

"Don't leave me," Amber said.

"Go on." And with a whoop of innocent glee, Samantha turned and swept at the wolf.

Amber did her best to run. She gasped and panted as the cramp in her side started to feel more and more like someone had broken one of her ribs and was pushing the jagged edge in against her organs. She kept her strides long and even as they had once been in her cross-country days. Her shoulders were now numb to the pain, and Johanna's weight had seemingly disappeared. Amber would have feared her niece lost to the fog if not for the swish of her windbreaker against the baby carrier's straps.

The fog grew thinner as she stumbled onward. Beyond the haze at its end, Amber could see the Otter Lake parking lot and the silhouette of the old, blue Ford. It was within reach, and she pushed a little harder, digging for what her track coach had called the last gasp. She nearly collided with the door of the truck as her frantic brain tried to command her weary body to stop. The silver tab inside the window told her she'd left the door unlocked. Amber wrenched it open, sweeping Johanna off her back and onto the front bench seat before scrambling in after her. She slammed the door shut and thumbed down the lock.

She could see the wolf hurtling out of the edge of the fog just a few feet away; wispy strands of vapor seemed to cling to its sides as it emerged from the woods. It was almost to the truck when the little girl appeared again. She ran at the wolf, arms wide open. They collided and tumbled back into the fog together, vanishing in an explosion of green mist. Clutching her niece tight to her chest, gurgling, hiccupping sobs tumbled out between Amber's breaths, penetrating the still, stale air of the truck's cab. She watched as the green mist dissipated amongst the rest of the grey fog like a congregation of lightning bugs departing into the night—each going their separate way.

LET HER GO

TREVOR O'HARA

When Susan left, my brother-in-law James took me out for dinner—
now my ex-brother-in-law. He took me to a steakhouse, his favorite,
and he got us a table in a corner in the back. The room was dark and
moody, and I felt there should be clouds of cigar and cigarette smoke
swirling around us while jazz music played. When the waiter came,
we immediately ordered drinks. For James, I suppose this was out if
habit, for me, discomfort.

James ordered a gin and tonic, and I ordered a beer. His order
seemed the more appropriate for the setting. The drinks came
quickly, and he started right in.

"She doesn't love you anymore, Nathan."

In a different situation, I might have thanked him for being blunt,
but I was feeling stubborn.

"Oh?" I said.

"Nathan"—he liked to call me Nathan instead of Natty or
Nate—"she's not happy, and she has the right to be happy."

I raised my beer and sipped.

"You don't agree?"

I put my beer down and thought for a moment, looking for a
trap. "She's my wife—" I started, but James cut in.

"And these are my clothes." He spread his arms to display his
very fashionable suit—he was a broker of some sort. "And this is

my drink." He raised his gin and tonic. "But when I finish my drink it's gone, and if I, God forbid, stain this suit during this meal, I'll have to buy a new one."

His metaphor made no sense, but it distracted me. "You would buy a new suit over one stain?"

"Oh, you can clean them, Nathan, but once stained, they're never quite the same."

I was speechless, and he took the opportunity to continue.

"When I went to prison"—he had done several months for some misconduct to do with his job—"the man I was with waited until I got home to tell me he was ending it. I thought it a strange thing for him to wait until I was out to do it, but he told me he didn't want me to lose hope inside, so he waited till I was free to break my heart."

"Were you heartbroken?" I asked, snidely. He had distracted me again, but I couldn't resist.

"Lord, no, Nathan. But you know how it is with men like myself, always a flair for the dramatic."

I was speechless again but finally found my voice.

"Jimmy"—he preferred James—"what does any of what you've said have to do with me and Susan?"

"I love my sister," he said, "and over the years, I've come to like you too, Nathan, and I want you to do the right thing."

"And that is?" I said.

"Let her go."

Susan had left me a week before, and this was not something I was prepared or wanted to hear. But he had disarmed me. He had stoked my emotions, removed them from the situation, and he had beaten me. I could say nothing more.

The waiter came again, James ordered for us both, and I let him. We ate mostly in silence, and after we were finished and James told me he would pay for the meal, we both stood, and he offered me his hand. I took it, we shook, and I left. James sat down again, I presumed to have another drink or three.

At home, I went to what had been our bedroom and picked up a vacation picture of Susan and me I had placed on my nightstand. I held it a time, looking at our smiling faces, then I walked it over to the dresser and stuck it deep in the bottom drawer under the clothes I didn't wear anymore.

I closed the drawer. I stood up, swore, then went to the kitchen for another beer.

CROSSING LINES

BRIANNA DOWDY

Larry Davis was flicking bread crumbs into the ocean.

He did this every Tuesday. Larry was an animal trainer, and while he enjoyed his job, he valued his days off—they were the only times he was able to watch creatures without having to direct their movements. If he had his way, the profession of animal trainer would not exist and he would be out of a job. Sure, he'd be destitute (he didn't know how to do anything else), but at least he wouldn't be associated with Siegfried and Roy.

However, animal trainers did exist, Larry did have a job, and flicking bread crumbs into the ocean was necessary for Larry to keep his sanity. Currently, he was aiming his crumbs toward a specific sea gull. It was a mother whose nest was nearby, and he was enjoying watching her gather up his crumbs and redistribute them to her chicks. He had been watching her for a good half hour. There was something about her selflessness that moved him, a quality he knew he lacked.

The gull wheeled above the surf, snatching a particularly large chunk of bread right out of the air. Larry laughed and ripped a few more pieces off, waiting for her to return. There were three chicks in her nest, and he loved watching them fight over the regurgitated bits of bread. One was particularly dogged and had a habit of stepping on the others. This made Larry giggle. Eventually though, even his tireless attention span waned, and Larry decided to go home. After all, SpaghettiOs wait for no man.

Roger was being difficult. Roger was a zebra being used in a new motion picture, and while Roger's part was not large, it was still important that he not look at the camera and flip his upper lip inside out every time the director called "Action!" Larry was nonplussed by this behavior; he'd been in the business for seven years and had never come across this before. Not in zebras. Still, he thought to himself, you learn something new every day. At least work wasn't going to be boring.

Finally, Larry was allowed to forget about Roger and go home. Usually Larry found only fleeting relief in this, but the zebra's antics today had tested him more than he was used to, and Larry found himself driving to his favorite beach five days ahead of schedule. There was still a little bit of daylight yet, and if he was lucky, his favorite gull hadn't already bedded down for the night.

Sure enough, there she was. He could tell her apart because one of her tail feathers was slightly ragged. This never affected her flying, but he wondered what had happened. Larry wasn't a particularly inquisitive person, and so the thought was brief, but it always came back when he saw her fly. Tonight, he saw that it—or something else—was actually making her list to the right. The light was starting to fade, and Larry squinted in an attempt to sharpen his vision. She was flying very erratically now, farther and farther from her nest. After a few dizzying seconds of trying to follow the bird across the sky, he saw the cause of her problems; a hawk was chasing her, and Larry watched, stricken, as the hawk made its final dive.

When the mother gull died, Larry felt as if the world went silent—even the crashing waves were muted. Then he heard the hawk start to tear into the bird, and it was too much. Larry shouted, ran forward and flapped his arms until the raptor took off, and then gathered up the fallen gull. As clichéd as it was, he couldn't help but note the frailness of the bird. She had seemed so feisty in life, and her stillness unnerved him. He took the body to the top of the outcropping where her nest was and began to bury her when a new thought came to him—her nest. The chicks were helpless. He finished taking care of the burial, put a large rock over the spot, and then dashed to his car. Larry may have been disgruntled, but that didn't make him lazy, and he hated to go anywhere unprepared. He found a large

Tupperware container and a fluffy dishtowel and then ran back to the outcropping.

Stuffing the towel into the container, making sure all of the plastic was covered, Larry inched out over the rocks toward the nest. When he got close, the chicks became absolutely silent—making themselves as small as possible and looking up at the giant, featherless creature named Larry with trepidation. Carefully, so as not to stress them any more than he had to, Larry gathered each of the chicks up and put them in the container, covering the top with a flap of towel he'd left out for that purpose. Larry then made his way back to his car, set the gull-filled Tupperware in his lap to keep them warm, and drove home.

The Tupperware sat on Larry's coffee table under a heat lamp while Larry frantically searched the Internet. He knew it was illegal to keep the babies himself, but had no idea where to take them. He had been searching for a half hour and had yet to find anything aside from local vet clinics (that would probably just euthanize the things anyway), and he was determined to find the birds a home. Exasperated, Larry leaned back in his chair and stared at his ceiling. If I were an orphaned wild animal, Larry thought, who would take me in? What kind of facility would have the resources to take care of wild baby birds? On a whim, he googled Galveston, TX zoo. A few clicks later, and he had found what he was after. Sure enough, the curator would accept orphaned wild animals, and the zoo would care for them until they were old enough to be released. There was a phone number on the page. Larry glanced at the time and winced. He would have to wait until the morning to phone in his Orphan Annies.

Larry parked his car and retrieved his precious cargo. At seven a.m. the zoo was oddly peaceful; it wouldn't open for another three hours, and the only people there were caretakers and other zoo employees. Larry stretched and took a step toward the side entrance. Suddenly, an alarm went off, and Larry could hear raised voices. He paused and looked at the container in his hands, but then curiosity got the better of him, and he went through the gate.

It seemed pandemonium had broken loose—along with a few of the lions. Normally, this wouldn't be a huge issue, but the man in charge of the lions was out sick that day, and no one knew exactly how to stop them from going wherever they damn well pleased. He looked once more at the gulls in his hands, then at the people panicking in all directions. He had come this far; he was not giving up now, not when he could actually do something about it. He set the gulls down beneath a shrub, out of the way of everyone falling over themselves, and approached the lions.

Two of them had gotten loose. The male wasn't really causing that much of a fuss—mostly he was just curious as to why everyone was being so loud. It was the female that had everyone nervous. She was much more active in her inquisitiveness and had roamed farther than her counterpart. Larry approached her first. With a few gestures and some body language, Larry managed to get her to lie down, then did the same thing with the male.

"Now stay there!" The employees watched in awe the entire time and applauded when the male sighed and collapsed onto the pavement. Larry nodded, blushing as he waved aside the praise. For once, he felt good about his profession, like he had actually accomplished something, but this was just a means to an end. He gathered up the chicks once more and proceeded to the curator's office, past the two offending felines.

Larry knocked and entered the small building only to find the curator frantically on the phone to the local authorities and completely oblivious to Larry's presence. He was a short, balding man in a smart suit with perspiration dripping down his shiny forehead. Larry cleared his throat, and the curator tore his ear away from the phone.

"What the hell do you want?"

Larry gestured to the container in his hands and explained the events. About halfway through the story, the curator had hung up on the police, but once Larry finished, he nodded grimly and redialed. Larry listened to the conversation with growing incredulity. Finally, the curator hung up once more, relieved Larry of the baby birds, and gestured for him to wait outside.

The squad car that had been on its way to deal with the lions was now there to deal with Larry. The policeman read Larry his rights, handcuffed him, and drove him to the station. Even if Larry hadn't had the right to remain silent, he would have. Speech had abandoned him. All he had wanted to do was help someone—something— other than himself. Despair wormed its way into his being. It's true, he thought as he stared at the vomit stain on the seat next to him, no good deed goes unpunished.

Three years later, Larry was making his familiar rounds. The company he had worked for previously had fired him in disgust, and since then he'd found it hard to find steady employment. This was his third apartment in as many months. The worst part was having to go door to door with his story and see the looks on people's faces.

Now, every time he passed a park, he carried a pocketful of rocks to throw at the pigeons. He avoided beaches altogether and had completely eliminated poultry from his diet. Every time he passed a police station, he swallowed his anger at the charge that had ruined his life and made him so bitter.

But as everyone knows, it is illegal to transport underage gulls across stayed lions.

SON OF A THOUSAND FATHERS

JOHN KENDALL

It's as simple as this: Bianchi has his gun pointed at Guevara, Guevara has his gun pointed at Rollins, and Rollins has his gun pointed at Bianchi.

But Bianchi isn't going down.

He watches Guevara's swarthy, round face, partially shaded by his filthy brown hat, and his eyes glowering at Rollins. He can feel Rollins's eyes affixed on him, as mortally as his gun. Behind Guevara, a tiny head appears in the window of a post office, like a sun dutifully rising from behind the mountains. A drift of dust floats by, and Bianchi tries to put it all out of his mind. There are only three things to focus on: his gun, Guevara's gun, and Rollins's gun. If he pulls his trigger, it certainly will be the end of Guevara, but Guevara will pull his trigger, Rollins will pull his, and a bullet will scream into Bianchi's skull and put him in the dirt.

"Looks like we got ourselves . . ." Guevara says with a devilish smile " . . . in quite the predicament."

Bianchi clenches his teeth at Guevara's arrogance. He wishes to God he had his pistol aimed at his smug smile rather than his temple, but any movement could mean the end. He feels a drop of sweat on his brow. He steadies his aim, fighting an ache in his arm.

Susan appears in Bianchi's mind. Susan with her auburn hair whipping in the wind and across her face. Susan with her silk skin and her sweetbriar cheeks. Susan standing in stalks of wheat, her yellow sundress hanging from her small breasts. Susan and her sultry voice, like a song from the seas. Susan who he will never lay eyes on again. The only thing he sees, the last thing he'll ever see, is Guevara's grimy, evil face. He's finished. No way out.

Bianchi feels the droplet of sweat begin to move down his brow toward his eye. It tingles as it moves, sending shivers through him. But he remains steady, calm. He doesn't shake. He doesn't shudder. He keeps his pistol pointed right at Guevara's head, in spite of its growing weight.

Footsteps and voices off to his right. Two women talking. Bianchi doesn't avert his attention. Guevara keeps his gaze affixed. Rollins's eyes continue to burn Bianchi's hair. The women suddenly gasp and scuffle about. Guevara snickers, and a door slams shut.

Bianchi's father appears in his mind. He's a tall, commanding man with an unconquerable stare. Bianchi sees his younger brothers. The ranch he grew up on. The red and yellow slews of paint in the sky from the sunset that came every night. His father, lying in the dirt, hands Bianchi his pistol, blood on its handle and his hands and waistcoat. His father whispers something to him that he doesn't hear. He gawks at the pistol. It's the pistol Bianchi draws quicker than Hendricks and Foster, the pistol that holds the bullets that drop all the bastards that draw down on him, the pistol that instills fear in anyone that gives him a shifty look. The pistol his father wasn't apt enough to wield. The very one that Bianchi now aims at Guevara.

Bianchi is getting out of this. He's seen tougher situations. His mother appears in his mind, but Bianchi shuts her away. There'll be time to think of her later. There'll be time for all of that later. Right now, he has to focus on the situation at hand.

The droplet of sweat on Bianchi's face stops at the corner of his eye. He moves his cheek, ever so slightly. The droplet continues down his face. The ache in his arm is immense. Bianchi ignores it. As soon as a distracting enough sound occurs—a door slamming, a horse neighing, window shutters bursting open—Bianchi will buckle his legs. He will drop toward the ground, throwing his head to the side. The guns will go off. Seeing as Rollins's arm isn't fully extended, when he shoots, the abruptness will cause his muscles to clench and he'll straighten his arm out as he's pulling the trigger, which will then cause the bullet to fly slightly high. It'll take off his hat and maybe a little scalp with it, possibly even rake his skull. But won't touch his brain. He'll live. Guevara's pistol will fire a bullet into Rollins's head, just above the ear, and into his brain. Bianchi's first shot at Guevara might not be a kill, but he'll have time for a second one as he's falling to the ground. Guevara will hit the dirt last, but Bianchi will be the only one left alive.

His mouth and throat are dry. He rubs his tongue on the roof of his mouth. It doesn't help. A ghostly wind creeps through the scene. It tickles the hairs on his face. It tugs at his hat. A slight tremor goes through his arm. His legs are growing tired. But he's surely not as tired as Rollins and Guevara. What was with Rollins's affinity for pulling corks? Bianchi's surprised the man's gun isn't shaking in his ear. And Guevara, seeing as holding onto a hand of cards and tossing poker chips aren't exactly muscle building exercises, he's nothing to worry about either. Any second now, one of them will falter, and Bianchi will have his moment. Those two poor, dumb bastards will be lying in their shallow, bloody graves.

Bianchi's not even sure either of them has ever killed a man. Perhaps Rollins. Maybe, in some drunken stupor, he got a shot off on some unfortunate bastard he mistook for a less than honest man. And Guevara, he would probably attest to killing a man or two—more likely a number higher than that—but he doesn't have the sand to actually take a man's life.

Dust sprinkles on their faces. Guevara flickers a cowardly arrogant eye, keeping the other open and steady on Rollins. Bianchi doesn't flinch. The droplet of sweat has made it to his chin. It barely tickles. Susan will greet him with such an embrace. She will kiss him so sweetly when he returns to her with but a minor scratch on his head. I was so worried about you honey, she'll say. There ain't nothing to worry about with me, baby, he'll reply and kiss her.

His finger clutches the trigger so tightly that it's getting sore. Rollins's pistol isn't drooping, isn't aiming any lower on Bianchi's head, giving him just a few more hairs of grace for when he dodges the bullet. Guevara—keeping his sneer unaffected—blows out the side of his mouth to get a fly off his face. Bianchi is calm. His heartbeat is controlled, steady. The wind settles. No more dust in his face. No breeze moving through his hairs. Or tugging at his hat. Just a perfect quiet as the droplet of sweat rests on Bianchi's chin—gravity pulling at it—and a horse neighs.

"Sam, get away from the window."

Sam looked back at his mother crouched in the corner with his younger sisters.

"Ma, they ain't going to shoot us," he replied, annoyed with his mother's coddling. "They got their pistols aimed at each other. We're fine."

He was on his knees, peering out the post office window at the three men in the street aiming their guns at one another.

"Still, son, a bullet might ricochet and come through the window."

Sam heard voices in the street and whipped his head around. He saw two lavishly dressed women walking down the way, gabbing and minding their own business. But when they saw the three men, they gasped and hid in the nearest building.

Sam returned his focus to the three men. He wanted Mr. Rollins to walk away from this, but knew that wasn't possible. Mr. Rollins was a dead man. The slightest movement and all three guns would go off. The only way for them to all walk away alive would be to talk it out, but Sam didn't see that happening. He'd witnessed his father die in a similar situation, and Mr. Rollins had been the closest thing to a replacement. He had seen to Sam and his family after his father was killed. He assisted with the family business and had said to Sam's mother that she'd convinced him to give up on the whiskey. At first, Sam hated how Mr. Rollins would give him that fatherly look and muss his hair, but he came to accept it as a gesture of approval and admiration. After all, Mr. Rollins did teach him how to shoot, how to draw. But he was a goner now. He probably deserved it too, on account of him being the drunken buffoon he once was and all the debaucheries he had no doubt got himself into.

"Samuel Albert Harris, you get over here right now!"

Sam whipped his head around.

"Ma, would you shut up! They're—"

A horse neighed, and there was a loud unison clapping sound. Sam almost jumped out of his boots. He whipped his head back to the window. Where just a moment ago there were three men standing in the street he saw three bodies dressed in useless clothes.

"Damn it," Sam muttered.

His mother scolded him for cursing as he got up, but she stayed, huddled in the corner with Sam's two whimpering sisters. He nearly knocked the door off its hinges as he stormed outside. A cool breeze covered the bodies with dust, as if the forces of nature were already fast at work on a speedy burial. Sam took in a breath and walked toward the mess.

"Sam, don't you go near them bodies," his mother called.

Off in the distance ahead of him, the doctor emerged trotting toward the bodies with his bag in one hand, the other holding his hat on his head. Sam got to the bodies just before the doctor did. They barely looked like men anymore.

The doctor examined them, and Sam thought him an idiot. He could clearly see holes in all three of their heads with spears of brain sticking out the back. What more diagnosis did it take?

"Get on out of here, son," the doctor said. "You don't want to be seeing this."

Sam glared at the man. He hated being called son, especially by men who weren't his father. Mr. Rollins had never called him son.

Sam unbuckled Mr. Rollins's belt and tugged at it until it came out from underneath his corpse.

"Now, what are you doin'?"

Sam ignored the doctor and wrapped the belt around himself. It sagged below his hips but he knew he would grow into it soon enough. He knelt down and picked up Mr. Rollins's pistol out of the puddle of red mud. There was blood on the pistol, and now on his hands, so he wiped it off on the coat of the blonde-haired man.

Sam took another look at the three pitiful dead men as blood from one of them crept toward his boots. He opened the loading gate of the pistol and turned the cylinder until he found the empty cartridge. He let it drop, and it made a plunk, landing in liquid. Sam pulled a bullet out of Mr. Rollins's bandolier, stuck it in the pistol, closed the loading gate, and vowed to be quicker, smarter, and a better shot than all three of these dead bastards. Come time he was grown, no life-desiring fool would dare draw down on Samuel Harris.

Sam flicked the gun's cylinder. It whirred as it spun until it came to a stop in the exact same position it had started. He put the gun in its holster. It made such a noise that the doctor jumped. Sam reveled in the doctor's small fear. He turned from the three dead men and walked away. He felt like a man. Felt taller. Closer to the sun.

THE STORM

ADRIENNE NICOLE

The car flew through the air quietly, snow and ice the least of the driver's concern. The storm unfolding outside had no effect on the cold serenity within.

"We'll live," she reassured the man.

"You always say that," he sighed. He looked out his window and sighed again, wondering why he was still thinking about her. A giggle echoed in his head, and he turned back to the vision of the girl.

"I don't need you. I don't know why you keep playing with me."

She frowned—a familiar, childlike pout—her round face exaggerating the expression and making her look deceivingly young. "Fine. Goodbye." And with that, she was gone. He imagined the passenger door hanging open and the sound of tires screeching to a stop ringing dully in his ears. He numbly got out of the car to look, because instinct told him it was the right thing to do. The girl was nowhere to be seen, of course. Maybe this time she wouldn't come back.

He got back in the car and sat in silence, dreading the quiet, wondering when he would see her next, afraid it wouldn't be long; that woman had a way of hanging around.

THE MONSTERS OF BAINBURY HILL

CHEYENNE MORSE

The new girl was weird. Millicent had not spoken a word since her arrival in Mrs. Dunn's fourth-grade class. She got by with gestures and a quiet that felt deep enough to drown in. It should have been impossible to spend a whole week in class and not talk to anyone. She never raised her hand. She never said please or thank you or can I sit next to you? She just lurked in the back corner, and nobody seemed to know what to do about it. She had to be some kind of freak, and the school had plenty of those already.

School was ending for the day, and it was Friday, so there was a restless shuffle in the room. When the bell rang, kids jumped up and started grabbing their gear out of their cubbies. Millicent leaned down and began sliding her books into her bag.

The sun that had been half blinding her through a bend in the plastic shutters over the windows suddenly vanished. When Millicent looked up to see what had blocked the sun, she saw three girls standing next to her desk.

"Your name is Millicent, right?" The girl with dark olive skin and dark hair cropped short asked. Millicent nodded.

"I'm Delaney, this is Kaida," Delaney said, she gestured to the blank-faced girl on her right who nodded in greeting, "and this is Lila." Delaney gestured to the dark-skinned girl on her other side. "We meet up on the west side of the building after school. You are welcome to join us. I feel it's only fair to tell you that we are monsters, but I don't think that's something that will worry you."

"We know you're one of us," Lila said. "You don't have to worry about fighting us, we've all recently eaten." She smiled and showed her canines, which looked quite sharp.

"We went hunting last night," Kaida said. Her voice was flat and clear like an undisturbed lake. The girls turned and left Millicent sitting where she was.

As she went out the door, Delaney smiled back at her. "Only if you'd like the company," she said over her shoulder.

Delaney, Kaida, and Lila waited by the west wall. The air was chilly, but it smelled like autumn. All of the girls breathed deeply. Kaida leaned against the wall while the others sprawled in the dying grass.

"Do you think she'll come?" Lila asked. Her windbreaker rustled as she hugged her knees to her chest. Her fingers plucked at her shoelaces.

"I think so," Delaney said.

"I wonder why she doesn't talk," Kaida said. "Do you think she's a siren?"

"No, I just get tired of people easily," Millicent said, coming up to stand with them.

"Not a problem with the likes of us," Delaney said, pushing herself to her feet. She brushed the dirt off her hands onto her jeans.

"Can we take her to the lake now?" Lila asked. She looked at Millicent. "It's the best place."

"It's a good place," Delaney said. "Would you like to see it?"

Millicent shrugged. Delaney took that as a yes and began to lead the way away from the school. It wasn't a quick walk, but the walk seemed to energize them. By the time they reached the lake, they were radiating energy.

There was moss on the stones, the water was a murky blue. It looked like the sort of place with stories buried at the base of every tree. The sort of place you would see ghosts. It would have been serene, but there were boys on the far shore tossing rocks into the water. When they saw the girls, they called out across the water.

"We were here first," the tallest one shouted.

"This place is ours," Delaney shouted back. "Get lost, or I'll hex you."

"This is my lake. No hexing," Lila said. She looked across the lake to the boys. "I'm going to eat anyone who's still there when I get over there." She kicked off her shoes and tossed her coat to the ground and dove head first into the lake.

Kaida stepped up next to Millicent. "Lila was born here at the bottom of the lake. It's special to her. Most everybody knows this is our place." Lila burst from the water on the far side. For a moment, her skin shimmered, and Millicent couldn't have said whether it was just water or the flash of scales. The boys were long gone. They'd started running the second Lila touched the water.

Lila gave herself a shake and then howled after the retreating shapes of the boys. The other girls joined in. After a moment, so did Millicent.

Lila continued swimming in the lake while Delaney spoke quietly to Kaida. Millicent sat on a log switching between getting lost in her own thoughts and watching the other girls. Kaida walked over to her and sat next to her.

"The others are curious, and that's why they will ask you questions. But it's okay if you don't want to answer them. I know people always say that it's okay if you don't want to talk, but these girls really mean it. It's okay if you're quiet a lot. I'm quiet all the time, and they don't mind." Kaida rubbed a silver-white scar on the back of her hand. "But you should know that if something in you is broken, Delaney is good at fixing things. She ate a witch's heart, she's pretty powerful." She tugged over the collar of her jacket and the shirt beneath it to show a long scar where her arm joined her shoulder.

"Since she put me back together, I can't be hurt anymore." Kaida unhooked a safety pin that had replaced a button on her flannel shirt. Without hesitation, she pushed it through the web of skin between her thumb and pointer finger. She held up her hand for inspection. Millicent reached over and grabbed Kaida's wrist.

"Stop that," Millicent said.

"It doesn't hurt at all, that's what I'm showing you. Nothing can hurt me."

"It doesn't matter if you can feel it or not. Never give up blood willingly. No one who cares about you would want you to hurt yourself. Anyone who wants to see you bleed should have to work for it."

"Okay," Kaida said. Millicent let go of her wrist, and Kaida pulled the pin from her hand. A bead of blood slid down her palm. Kaida licked it up with a quick dart of her tongue. She licked the blood off the safety pin as well and pinned her shirt back together.

Kaida nodded to Millicent, then got to her feet. She wandered to the edge of the lake and stood there, though whether she was looking at her own reflection or at something deeper in the water, Millicent couldn't tell. After a few minutes, Lila's head bobbed above the surface. She waved a hand at Kaida, beckoning her into the water. Kaida shrugged off her coat and shoes and waded into the lake until the water closed over her head.

"She's taken an interest in you," Delaney said from behind Millicent. "That's unusual. She usually doesn't take an interest in anything."

"I don't know if it's that." Millicent looked over her shoulder at Delaney and then back out across the water. "She thought maybe I didn't talk because I was broken."

"She didn't mean anything by that," Delaney said, but Millicent waved the concern away.

"I've been broken before. Everything breaks eventually. What happened to her?" They looked over the water to where Lila and Kaida were splashing water at each other.

"A car accident. A really bad one. They thought she was dead. I heard her scratching around in her coffin and dug her up, sewed her back together."

"Are graveyards the best place for heart eating?" Millicent asked with what almost looked like a smile.

"She really has been talking to you. Yeah, I spend time out in the graveyard. It's a good place. For a long time, I thought I'd fixed her up good as new, but she's been a bit off. I thought maybe I missed a piece of her when I dug her out of the dirt, but it's her heart. Her mom was in the same accident as she was. There were a lot of doctor's visits, she hurt all the time, it made her bitter. As soon as her mom could walk again, she just kept walking and never came back. I think it broke Kaida's heart, and I'm not really one for fixing hearts."

Eventually, Kaida and then Lila were coaxed out if the water. After they had wrung as much water out of themselves as they could, the girls all walked away into the trees. There was a steep slope beyond, and they set to climbing it. The four of them scrambled upward. At some point, each of them had to stoop to all fours to make it. Rocks slithered away from their footholds, tumbling back down toward the lake. When they reached the top, they were all panting.

"What now?" Millicent asked.

"Kaida's house, it's closest," Lila replied. They approached from the back of the house, and they climbed over the fence rather than walk around to the front. The back doors were glass, and they slid easily open when Delaney yanked sideways on the handle.

"Is that the pitter-patter of monstrous feet?" a male voice called out.

"We're here, Mr. Fletcher," Delaney called back. There were several towels hanging from the back of the kitchen chairs. Lila started scrubbing herself dry. Kaida just dripped as she wandered through the kitchen. A man, tall and lanky, came around the corner into the kitchen. There was no question in Millicent's mind that this was Kaida's father. They shared the same hair color, and they both tilted their heads in exactly the same way when they looked at her.

"Is this a new visitor?" He asked, his easy smile almost erased any of the similarities between them.

"This is Millicent. She's new in our class," Delaney explained. Kaida's father walked over and took one of the towels from a chair and covered Kaida's hair with it. He scrubbed it around, drying her hair and wiping her cheeks with the edges.

"No twigs in your hair today, I hope," he said down to his daughter, smiling.

"I told you, Dad," she said, her voice muffled by the towel, "the twigs and mud are just for special occasions, like Halloween."

"Of course, how could I forget?" He removed the towel. Beneath it, Kaida's hair was a tangled mess. "Isn't it getting a little cold for the lake?"

"No," Kaida said. Her lips were blue, but she wasn't shivering.

"So are you a monster as well?" Mr. Fletcher asked Millicent while he tried to get Kaida's hair to behave. "Or just a brave human?"

"Actually, I'm a wandering spirit. When I find a person who is empty inside, I take them over so I can have a physical body."

"A solid plan. If wandering spirits still need sustenance, there are some sandwiches of indeterminable origin in the fridge," Mr. Fletcher said.

"And blood," Delaney said, as she pulled a pitcher of red liquid out of the fridge.

"I'll take some," Lila said as she dried herself off. After a moment's hesitation, Millicent asked for a glass as well. All four girls sat at the table with their drinks. Lila and Kaida were at least dry enough not to drip water on the floor anymore. Mr. Fletcher put the sandwiches on the table.

"I'll take these towels upstairs. Just shout if you need anything." He winked at Millicent and left the kitchen with an armload of damp towels.

Over the course of her friendship with the monster girls, Millicent would meet all of their parents. It became apparent very quickly that even if Kaida's house had been the farthest away, they would have still gone there.

It was the middle of the night, and Millicent was sneaking out of her window. She'd never done anything like it before, but she didn't feel guilty about it. The only thing that had been stopping her was that she'd simply had nowhere to go. Tonight, she was meeting the girls on the hill two blocks from their school, Bainbury Hill. The moon was full, so there was plenty of light to see by. She walked. There wasn't far to go. In fact, she beat Lila and Delaney there, but only by a few moments. Kaida was already on the hill. Millicent was still climbing to the top of the hill when the other two biked into the parking lot.

"It's a good night for this," Kaida said, extending a hand to help her friend to the top. "The moon is bright. Sometimes it's too cloudy. You must be good luck."

"Do believe in that? Luck?" Millicent asked. Kaida shrugged.

"It's something people say. Things seem better with you around, like it's always the full moon."

"That is a really nice thing to say," Millicent said with a smile.

"I may not feel things, but I know things. I can see that the others are happy that you are here too."

"This is the happiest I've ever been," Millicent said. They both stared up at the moon. In the moment of quiet that followed, they could hear the other girls chatting on their way up the hill. There was a light layer of snow on the ground, so Lila and Delaney held hands to keep each other from slipping back down to the bottom.

"We should go north tonight, it's been a while." Lila was saying.

"It's Millie's first moon," Delany replied. "She should get to choose." The girls stumbled to the top.

"We're all here. What do we do now?" Millicent asked.

"Full moons are for hunting," Lila said. "But first—" She threw back her head and howled. All four of them threw back their heads and howled. Their breath steamed in the air, curling around them like a fog. When they were panting and breathless and grinning uncontrollably, Lila put her arm around Millicent's shoulders and gave her a squeeze.

"What looks like the best way to go?" she asked. Millicent smiled at her, stepped forward, and spun wildly in a circle. The hill was so slick that she almost stumbled and fell, but Kaida grabbed the back of her jacket and kept her from going down. Millicent thrust out an arm, still too dizzy to see clearly.

"North!" Lila cried happily. She led the charge back down the side of the hill. All four of them were howling again, their red mouths turned up to the sky.

The first semester was ending, and all the windows were frosted over. The whole class was gathering their belonging. Mrs. Dunn came to stand by Kaida's desk.

"Kaida, I would like to speak to you for a couple of minutes. Alone, please." Delaney looked at her friend to make sure she was okay with this. Kaida nodded, and the others reluctantly left her on her own. Once they were alone in the classroom, Mrs. Dunn began speaking.

"I wanted to talk about your grades. I know things have been really difficult for you since your accident, and I know that you have come a long way in a short time, but I'm concerned that you might not be prepared to move forward next year. After you spent so much of last year out of class, I know some were hesitant to move you forward. Your father said you would do better if you could be with your friends, and I see how you are together. I'm so happy that you girls care so much about each other, but it's just as important to understand the material that you are being taught. I know that you are very intelligent, and I know that you can do all of this work, you just need to apply yourself."

She paused and studied Kaida's face, looking for some flicker of acknowledgment, but there was nothing.

"There is still time in this year, and I'm happy to work with you as much as you'd like. Do you understand what I'm saying?" Mrs. Dunn asked. Kaida nodded. "Do you have any questions for me?

Anything you want to talk about?" Kaida shook her head. "Alright, that's all for today, just remember you can talk to me about anything."

"Yes, Mrs. Dunn," Kaida said. She collected her things and went out of the classroom. The other girls were waiting for her in the hall.

"Is everything okay?" Delaney asked. Kaida shrugged but after a moment told them what Mrs. Dunn had said.

"That's stupid," Lila said.

"Would you like a hug?" Millicent asked.

"It would be wasted on me," Kaida said.

"You might not be able to feel, but you'll know," she replied. Kaida considered this for a moment and then opened her arms. Millicent embraced her. Kaida even closed her arms around Millicent in return.

The lake was frozen over, but that didn't stop the girls from visiting it almost every day after school. Lila bounced rocks off the top of the ice. She hollered in victory anytime she managed to get it to crack.

The trees were snowy and spattered with ice, but that didn't keep the girls from climbing them. Delaney was perched between two sturdy branches reading to them out of the book they had been assigned for school, pausing every now and then for Lila's victory shouts. Millicent and Kaida were in the tree next to her, trying to see how high they could get on the slick branches.

"My butt is freezing," Delaney said, shifting uncomfortably. She pulled herself to her feet by grabbing a branch above her. She nearly had her balance before the branch snapped in her hand. Her arms flung out, but she wasn't able to grab anything sturdy enough to hold her.

Millicent leapt down from above and swung out on the longest limb so she could grab Delaney's arm. There was a moment when the only sound was the creaking of branches because all the girls were holding their breaths.

With a shove from Millicent, Delany was able to grab a hold of the main trunk of her tree. She wrapped both her arms around the trunk, and everyone breathed a sigh of relief.

There was another loud snap, and the branch that was holding Millicent's weight gave. She and the branch fell through the air. Everyone froze in shock, everyone but Kaida, who began to climb down the tree.

Millicent was laid out on the ground, unmoving. She was cracked like a porcelain figure. There was no blood, white steam escaped where she was broken. Kaida got to her first. Kaida held Millicent tightly and gently.

"Hold on, you're going to be okay. You're going to be okay." She pressed her hands over the biggest cracks, trying to stop Millicent from floating away to nothing.

"You can use my body, you'll be safe in here, it will take good care of you," Kaida told her.

"I can only use an empty vessel."

"Delaney can eat my heart. There isn't much of me in here, you can have it."

"You aren't empty, you are full and deep and beautiful."

Kaida leaned her forehead against Millicent's and began to weep. With a sound like broken ceramic pieces rubbing together, Millicent raised a hand to cup Kaida's cheek. At that moment, it was impossible to tell who was consoling whom.

"I will find a new vessel as soon as I can, and I will find you again," Millicent said, her voice sounded like it was coming from very far away. Delaney knelt next to the two girls, Lila remained standing, perched on her toes like she was going to run for help at any moment. But she wouldn't leave her friend's side right now. There wasn't time for anything but goodbye.

"Every full moon," Lila said, "we will be on the hill."

"No matter what, we will be there," Delaney said.

There was now only a thin stream of mist curling out between Kaida's fingers.

"I'll look for you."

Then she was gone.

Their parents didn't let them go to the funeral, but that didn't matter to them. They all knew the way to the graveyard, and they preferred to pay their respects on their own. They believed Millicent was out there, searching for a way to back to them. However, the broken thing buried in her grave had served as her home, if only for a little while, and it needed a proper farewell.

They went at night, when the moon was high. It was not full, a piece of it was carved away by darkness—just like them, a piece lost to the night.

Each of them had thought to say something, but in the end, silence seemed the only appropriate thing. They set gifts for Millicent on the base of her gravestone like they were laying them at her feet, not resting them on the dirt her pieces were buried under.

Delaney brought dirt from the witch's grave whose heart she had eaten. Lila brought stones from the bottom of her lake—she always kept a few in her room so she never felt far from home. Kaida brought a vile of her tears. The blue glass of it caught the moonlight, and it shimmered. After setting their gifts in front of her headstone, they stood around the grave until a cloud covered the moon. Then they left the graveyard and walked off toward Bainbury Hill. They felt the need to raise their voices.

They howled at the moon, and the long, sad notes hung together in the night air.

They returned the following week to stand beneath the full moon and sing that ancient song that all wolves and monster know. They returned for every full moon thereafter, and each month, the song grew louder and more joyful. Each month, it was more likely that the final voice they were waiting for would rise up along with theirs, and they would finally be complete.

THE COWBOY

TEEKA A. BALLAS

"If you sit still long enough," my father would say, his voice drawn out, long, slow, low as the bottom of a gravel pit, "you'll most certainly be privy to secret displays of magic." He'd first wink his left eye, a laying down of long lashes across high cheekbone, then twist the ends of his mustache with thick index fingers and thumbs, a single stroke of his beard with one hand like the final wring of moisture from a wash rag, then lean back as far as his chair would allow him.

"What magic have you seen?" I'd ask, always midstride. Surely he'd seen his share; my father was not one to move fast or often.

"There's a difference between sitting still and lazing about," my mother would chide from the other room while sewing on buttons, taming horses, charting stars.

His eyes would narrow into a scowl, then fling open like a wide laugh, throwing light into the corners. If I wasn't in transit, moving too fast, midfight with a flock of angry dragons, I'd come down from the ceiling, curl up in to the shadow of his lap, listen closely to his tales: soft, dry volcanic ash falling from his lips, blanketing me with what my mother and I knew to be challenges to reality. Our adoration could not be apprehended. It was an exaltation, a declaration, a mandate from the universe issued upon us as keepers of trysts and tribes and binding ties. We would do anything, use any tool or artifact to make tangible the magic he'd attest to: bicycle pump, fish net, landing pad. If his magic was real then so were we.

"Never rely on your foot in the stirrup," my father'd say. "You never know when the horse might bolt or buck or just decide to hip check you into the air." I don't think he ever rode a horse. Most likely no roper would know what in tarnation he was talking about. "Listen for clues," he'd whisper conspiratorially. "Press your hand to its muzzle, feel for the rumble." My father was a cowboy.

For hours, I have been reclining in the shadow of the sunshine, soaking up its lethargic rays, waiting for a ride to come along and offer me a rollie and a change of scenery. I lean back in my roadside easy chair, beneath the on-ramp NO HITCHHIKING BEYOND THIS POINT sign, where hitchhikers before me have emblazoned on the back of the sign their names, their destinations, and their miseries—acts of defiance against law, order, and monotony. I contemplate the stagnation of time versus travel. I have spent from day to dawn counting grains of sand, teaching myself the melodic compositions of silence, notating the seconds that fill stillness, recalling my father's orations. A breeze so subtle it is impossible to discern the direction of its origin throws the grains of sand I've counted and lined up on the ground beside my left foot: one million five hundred thirty-six—scattered. I hear my father whisper through tight creases, like the flash of streak lightning on the far horizon— impossible to tell if it's approaching or retreating.

I am just beginning to nod off when I hear a scuttle of stones, and my head snaps up. There's a ringing in my ears, and I'm temporarily blinded as I open my eyes into the sun.

A suspicious, somewhat nefarious looking character is approaching me. He has an itchy walk and a twitch in his eye—the kind that comes from running into too many slammed doors. I lean harder against my rucksack, take mental inventory of my must haves and don't haves, and grab the empty sheath at my hip.

The perspiration of anticipation laced across my face turns cool with the ignominy of my erroneous judgment as I get a closer look. The dusty stranger is nothing more than a cowboy. The old-fashioned, storybook, western-fairy-tale, guitar-slingin', blues-singin', trustworthy kind, with worn hat, tarnished boots, torn britches, and a bottle of Tabasco sauce at the hip. If a movie were to be made about my father, this character here would surely play him.

I didn't have to wait long, but the olfactory details of that wait lay on a timeline that was immeasurable, yet surely infinite: the smell of refuse, dust, impossibly long rays of sunshine, and hiccups of choked tears.

Long waits for rides are like hosting parties with a strong reliance on strangers attending: up until they arrive, you're sure no one is going to come—it's not until they're all gone and you've got your home to yourself again do you know if inviting strangers was such a good idea. This is why when I wait for a ride, I practice dragon slaying. And bartending.

As I can recall, the VW bus was identical to one my mother had a photograph of with me siting in it, six years old, a grin from hairline to hairline, arm around our German shepherd, chocolate smeared across my face. The bus was mustard yellow with brown panels, orange and brown interior. My mother hated that shade of yellow, said it was the color of a baby's shit after eating meat and peas. I, however, having been nearly a baby at the time, revel in the memory, those colors the warmth of safety, security, dragon-free skies, and freshly changed diapers.

The driver was Frog, a tiny young woman with a shock of red hair, splattered freckles, and a smile that surpassed the circumference of her face. She didn't even ask me where I was going. She just told me to get in. It was clear she and her companions were going wherever I was going to go—I was just along for the ride.

"This is Rainbow," she said, passing a bottle of Tabasco to a delicate young woman in layers of long flowing skirts, her hair braided with ribbons and shells. Rainbow took a loud, rambunctious gulp from the bottle of spicy sauce and passed it to the woman beside her. "That's Destiny," Frog said. Destiny too had long hair braided with random artifacts and string, her skin the shade of night when all light has been filtered out of the sky.

"You look like you've been on the side of the road for a long time," Destiny said to me. "Need some?" She leaned forward to hand me the bottle, and her fingers lightly brushed mine.

"I . . . uh," I stammered, unable to control the blush across my face. "It's a little early for me." I was not ready to fully confess.

Destiny shrugged, passed the bottle, and leaned back against her pack and eyed me suspiciously.

"That's Chante." Frog pointed at the woman who took the bottle from Destiny. Chante did not look at me. She was staring off into a zone between me and Frog. She passed the bottle back to Destiny, and her hands went back to reading a book on her lap, her fingers light atop the pages.

"And that's Hope," Frog said, pointing to a young Hawaiian. Her thick, black hair cut just above the shoulders looked as though it had been sawed off with a steak knife. She was lying on the top bunk, her face pressed up against the glass, looking back at where we'd come from. She too did not acknowledge me. She too did not take a sip off the bottle.

"Howdy!" he says with a curtsy of his hat. "Can I's be offerin' ya some Tabaski for the ol' achin' throat there?"

"No thanks," I say, "that stuff's a little too hot for me." I'm still embarrassed to admit my lack of fortitude and strength. "Got a smoke, though?"

"Nope. Cain't says that I do, Miss. You shouldn't be doin' that anyways. Last I 'eard, smokin' kills."

"Yeah, well they say just about anything free thinkers do is lethal. I suppose anything that entails living is pretty much guaranteed to be bad for you."

He chuckles and kicks at the dust. "Ain't no doubt about it." A pause. "Say," he says, peering down at my feet through his thin slit, dirt-encrusted eyes, "you've got some gnarly boots goin' on. Looks like they've got a few bullet holes in 'em. You's a cowboy too?"

"Well, not really. More like a—just a horse that doesn't want to be lassoed. I don't think I'll ever have what it takes to be a cowboy." It's been humbling to learn and come to terms with the fact that I may walk among them, but I will never be one of them. This is the first time I've admitted this out loud.

"What exactly is a cowboy?" he asks me, with pure, unadulterated naiveté—ironically, the kind that genuine rough-and-tumble cowboys are renowned for. He reminds me of a man, etched and engraved in my childhood memories, who also had possessed such sincere innocence.

"You should know! You are a cowboy, aren't you?"

"Well, that's what they's say, but it ain't nothin' I n'ever strived ta be. If I is, then it musta jist sorta happ'ned 'thout my knowin' it."

"Well," I say, as I pull my knees up to my chin and recite to him with well-rehearsed authority, "the way I've heard it told, cowboys are stones smoothed over by long, slow-moving streams. They will stomp on any ground regardless of its condition, with the soles of their well-worn boots soaking up all the pain as well as all the glory of those who have preceded their footfall. Cowboys have no need for material things and are always forgetting to take care of the little they do possess. Because of this, they tend to be horrid roommates and frightful spouses. A cowboy likes to sit beneath the brim of his hat, shielding his eyes from the glare of the sun as he peers out at a world succumbing to profanity and greed. A cowboy has a passport to the world—the kind that can only be obtained once the soles of the feet have been indicted for neglect and overuse. And a cowboy lives for the spicy taste of life . . . the stuff that burns your tongue and stings your eyes. The stuff that keeps you alive." I point to the bottle of Tabasco sauce tied to his waist. "Looks like you're a one-hundred-percent-certified, positively bona fide, absolutely guaranteed, official, real-life cowboy."

The cowboy chuckles and tips his hat up a little bit further. He eyes me with deep brown eyes, dark and gold like his skin, a long, solidifying stare, and tilts his head—a hawk amused with the frantic scurrying of a field mouse. I am uncomfortable beneath his gaze but not threatened. "What? Did I miss something? Are you challenging me?"

"No, Miss. I jist don't believe I've e'er heard no one spill it like that." He flashes me a wide, stained-tooth grin.

"Well, now you have. So, since the evidence is clear that you are not a roadside serial murderer, have a seat here beside me and privilege me with your presence."

The cowboy nods his head and, like a resurrected dinosaur, falls into place beside me.

We talk and think about talking and wade along comfortable silences through immeasurable days and nights, holding hands and exchanging experiences, until he catches a ride heading in the opposite direction that I am. Once again, I am alone, idling over memories and cognizance, charting stars and counting clouds, whistling Doo Wah Diddy Diddy and Yellow Submarine, cleaning my nails and picking my teeth, waiting for a ride going my direction to finally come along. My hand is still warm and recollecting the softness of his fingers wrapped in mine.

"I was about your age when I started hopping trains," my dad blurted out. He toyed with bread crumbs on the table, not looking me in the eye or into the filament between us—which was highly unusual for him.

It had been an unbearably long afternoon, every strand of shade being choked by fat rays of boorish sun. Even cicadas were down for a nap. A condensation puddle from my glass of lemonade had begun to rivulet off the edge of the table and down my leg. It was mildly refreshing but fully evaporated by midcalf.

"Hmm?" I asked, words too heavy to pick up and lay out in front of me. My mother sat between us filling crossword boxes with ink. She cleared her throat—it sounded like a warning, the subtle kind, like when you want to gently remind someone not to step on a crack lest you break your mother's back.

He looked up at her from beneath a hedge of eyebrows, assessed possible damages, and continued: "I needed to get somewhere fast."

"Fast? Why not drive a car? Ride a bike? Catch a flight?" I was barely invested in him that afternoon.

He stole a glance at my mother who was devoutly bent to the task of ignoring him. "The train takes the route of the crow. It steals old men's dreams as it rushes through towns at the midnight hour and harbors new ones in the imagination of children. It's the fastest way to put distance between you and your demons without leaving a paper trail of evidence."

"What were you running from?" It was hard to imagine my father running. As long as I'd been alive, he'd never run to or from anything. He couldn't.

"Let's just say it was an entry point—an exit from a life that was distracting and a bridge into the land where sitting still reveals not a lack of fortitude but an indulgence of wonderment and awe. Awe is at the source of it all. Awe is what reveals the true character. Without awe, there is no reason to stare at sunsets, count stars, dance with ghosts, catch snowflakes, make wishes on comets, fall in love."

"What is awe?"

"When your breath is stolen by the weight of what your eyes

behold."

"When have you felt awe?"

"When I met your mother." My mother sighed loudly and put her pen down, but did not look up. "And when you were born," he said proudly.

"What else has stolen your breath?"

"The first time I saw fairies."

"Like real, live, living fairies?"

"In an empty box car still fresh with the smell of horse and feed. There must have been thousands of them, all lit up, glowing like fireflies low flying over slow moving river water. Saved my life, they did. I'd been hurt bad. Could have died. Yup."

My mother sighed again and placed one of her hands atop one of his.

"What've ya learned since last I seen ya's?" he asks, rubbing his hands together over the roadside campfire I've built from weary grass, tumbleweeds, and fast food bags.

"That everything I write is symbolic of everything that surrounds," I say, chewing an itch on my bottom lip.

"Whadjya write?" he asks, sitting back and taking a swig off his hot sauce.

"Nothing," I say. He offers me a swig off the bottle, but I decline.

We stare out at the storm gathering on the horizon, not thinking about what I've written or symbolisms but about ventures and endeavors. The storm approaches, and he is gone again, like the last credit at the end of a great picture show, picked up by someone going his way, leaving me to sit in the dust that abounds, waiting to find my direction.

It had started with a pop and then a bang, a shudder, and a swerve. Frog and Destiny hopped off the bus to assess the damage. A flattened tire.

"It's the third one in a month! I'm going to hitchhike into town and grab a new tire. Rainbow, why don't you come with me. And Destiny, you can stay here and watch over things," announced Frog. She didn't need to say it. We all knew she and Destiny were the toughest, dust-slingin'est, Tabasco-drinkin'est cowgirls in the bunch. "Don't know how long it will take—maybe a day?" Destiny stood behind Frog glaring at me. She said something to her that sounded fiery with accusation. Frog shook her head and clapped her on the shoulder. "I read her dreams. Don't worry about it."

I didn't know what that meant, but Destiny did. She crawled back onto the bus and sat down on the kitchen couch beside me. Rainbow and Frog grabbed bottles of water and day packs and set off.

Throughout the event—the popping tire, the swerving vehicle, the cloud of dust as we came to a halt on the side of the road—Chante had not looked up from her book. Hope had sat silently staring at the orange shag carpeting, hugging to her chest a long, narrow pink box. She'd been holding it since the last town where she had, with the box in hand, marched off with a purpose but returned before dark with a deeper crease in her forehead.

Destiny, in a radical change in temperature and posture, scooted over to me on the couch, and pointed with her forehead in the direction of Hope. "It's her hair."

I looked at her quizzically.

"In the box. She tries to sell it in every town. Chante cut it for her. The most beautiful hair you've ever seen. Says she used to wash it with avocados that she picked in her backyard." Destiny's thick coffee voice was rich with awe.

"Why did she cut it?" The severing sounded as impossibly awful as the specter that my father had told me about, the one who stole his legs—in some tellings it was an alligator.

"She has demons. Demons woven into her hair." I'd always thought of demons and monsters as being interchangeable.

Destiny told me about Hope's demons. They were not like the kind I'd always imagined—the kind that follow you around like a small bird prematurely fallen from the nest, vying for your attention, barking at you to regurgitate a worm for them. Not the kind of friendly monster-demons that helped you slay dragons when your sword proved futile. The kind of demons Hope had I did not know existed—they were the kind that haunted even her best of dreams.

I wondered for the first time about the demons my father spoke of. It had never occurred to me that his monsters were not all friendlies. I dozed off and dreamt of my father fighting off Hope's demons with a posse of his own friendly monsters and poisoned-dart-wielding fairies.

When I awoke, we were blanketed in darkness. Destiny was curled up comfortably in the crook of my left arm. A soft rustling came from the bed in the back. In the glow of a pink effervescent light, I could see Hope bowled over in silent, racking sobs. Chante sat beside her, one hand placed atop her head, the box of hair open on her lap.

The light was slowly pouring out Chante's mouth and beginning to fill the entire bus. On each ray of light, I ascertained a slender naked being, hip bones jutting out, shoulder blades of sharpened knives, and knees round balls atop slender sticks. As they glided down from Chante's mouth, they landed atop the open box, unraveled a strand of hair each, wrapped them like a turban around their heads, and elevated into the open, sobbing mouth of Hope.

Fairies.

I knew I must be dreaming, but I'd never felt closer to my father, safer in this world because of him.

"Why're ya cryin'?" he asks.

"Because your hot sauce brings tears to my eyes."

"Maybe ya shouldn't be sippin' Tabasco then. Maybe sweets're better to yer likin'," he says.

My fists start to ball up. He has no idea what I like. What I want. What I need.

He shrugs, sensing my building anger. He has conflict aversion. He puts his hot sauce back in its sheath and rises, stirring up dust that has been sleeping since I first left home. "You got a lot ta figure out 'fore ya can drink the sauce without blisterin' from its sting." Before I have time to contemplate and reply, he is gone yet again, leaving the dust to settle back into place, taking up the space of silent memories. And like each time before, I shed tears for the divestiture of his affection, his absence a grief embracing my dusty knoll.

"I see yer skirts're torn," he says. He does not seem to harbor any resentment or memory of our last altercation. "You been travelin' hard?"

"Nah," I say, "I haven't left this dusty, crusty, sorry excuse for a hitchhiking post since last I saw you."

"Then how've ya worn yer dress so?"

"I don't know. Maybe it's the glare of the sun, or the brute force of the constantly nagging wind. Maybe it just appears that way."

"Many things are exactly as they appear," he whispers into my hair, almost a kiss, his lips brushing the tips of my ears.

*

This time, I do not cry when he embarks on his new quest. Instead, I look into the fading sunset that whispers only phony promises of forever and recollect the time my father told me a story of how he hopped a train thinking it would take him from Phoenix to Seattle, and instead it took him to New Orleans. I wonder at what point did he realize he was headed in the wrong direction.

"Have ya travelled far?" he asks, rubbing a dry, chapped hand over his scraggly chin, giving my discarded boots a scrutinizing gaze.

"Nah," I say, scratching the bottoms of my under-calloused, over-rested, dry, itchy feet. "It has had to come to me instead."

"So yer a cowboy now," he says, looking truly tired and fatigued, smoke from disenchantment browsing his hair. He looks a lot like my father would when he'd return home from wrangling horses in the corral, or wrestling rattlers in the dried creek bed: weary, but deeply satisfied.

"What is a cowboy?" I ask, pulling my boots back on. I can hardly seem to recollect the specifics.

I watch as he disappears—a lonely, distant silhouette, etched into colors that imitate sunsets long since faded, looking like the backdrop to an old celluloid masterpiece. His disappearing silhouette is reminiscent of my father's.

I have not seen the cowboy in a long time. Perhaps he's run out of Tabasco or he's had to hang his hat. "We will meet when our paths cross again," I whisper aloud, hoping a stray dust devil might pick up my request and send it to someone who's in control of delegating wishing and receiving. But the air is flat and devoid of movement, leaving me to wish silently for more control over fate and paths. I gather my crusty things and get into the waiting automobile, my first ride in a very long time, and wave good-bye to the space I leave behind.

I sit back in the front seat of the blue four-door Escort and stare at my new pair of deep maroon suede boots, nary a particle of dirt upon them. Destiny looks over at me, pushes a loose strand of hair behind her ear, and smiles a grin the size of Florida. She grinds and shifts into gear, then takes my hand in hers. I shut out the hyper chatter in my mind and reflect on my time served and try to replay images of the cowboy. Instead, I get my father in wide-screen format and Dolby surround sound. I lean against the door and listen to the audio in my head replay the dozens of tales my father spun. He once told me of a girl he met hitchhiking, how she did it all by herself with nothing but a rucksack and a canteen. I try to imagine what kind of canteen she had as I remove the bottle of Tabasco from the pocket at my hip and take a long, hard swallow.

I pass it to Destiny. For a minute, I think she is going to pass it to my father, who is wrapped up in a cat tangle with Hope in the back seat, thick as thieves. We both know it would be foolish. One of them would surely spill it.

END SCENE

ELIZABETH WEISSBERG

They're going to kill us, these humans circling our camp. We don't know how or when. It'll probably be soon. For now, they're saying no more than the trees at their backs.

I look to my left, to Mitsy, her hologram of skin there and then not, the way it does when she gets nervous. Her insides are beautiful, seventeen parallel rods in shining coppers, platinums, and golds, doing everything needed to keep her going.

The humans keep circling. The skin on their faces hangs over itself, and their expressions are dour. We hear footsteps from beyond the trees, in the direction of a lake plump with surface tension.

My artificial breath catches in my throat. It's him. We've thought he was dead for so long. No one has ever escaped the humans' trackers. His projection body has changed. It's plump and squished in the middle, and his face is flabby and unshaven. He looks like one of their vagrants.

The humans stop circling. They stand and listen to what he says. He's been travelling alone. He hadn't known what it would be like to be alone, disconnected, and now he does. He's slept with a human woman, halfway across the world. I hurt a little at this. I have questions at this. But I know the time to ask is later.

I walk up to him, just gaze at him, and am filled with an urge to sob at how much I love him and have missed him. I can feel his love reflect back on me. He hasn't yet put down his traveler's pack.

The humans retreat. Their footsteps on the dried leaves disappear into nothingness. He's needed to make no show of strength. The humans understood he would win.

I back away so he can focus on the others. Between exchanges, he sometimes disappears into the forest, and Vanessa is angry at him because he doesn't explain why he's doing this before he greets her. Her ability to be irritated rather than awestruck by how everything has suddenly changed makes it just like old times.

I feel so much gratitude, I am filled with the need to sob again. Back to normal is all I've longed for.

AN ANNOTATED LIST OF WAYS BY WHICH YOU CAN SKIP TOWN

PETER BRADLEY

1. Car

If you own a car, take it. If you don't, the best option is hitchhiking. Position yourself near highway exits and wait. Try to not be afraid of hitching, then be afraid anyway. Be more afraid of failing.

When a car with a Jesus fish stops, get in. They ask where you're going, and you tell them anywhere but here. They laugh, you don't, and the silence after is awkward.

They ask about your job, you tell them you quit. They ask about family, you tell them you'd rather just not. They ask if you're in trouble, and you try to explain you won't know if you're in trouble until you get to where you're going, and you don't know where you're going. You say sometimes you feel like you can see the place where everything will be okay, and you put your head down and move toward it, but by the time you look back up, it's behind you, so you repeat, and it happens again.

You take a deep breath, and they ask if you're on drugs, and they tell you their church has a great program for "kicking the monkey off your back."

You ask them to please pull over. By then it's dark, and no one will stop.

The walk home is pleasant. Your fiancé has made eggplant

parmesan with lentils. She asks about your day. You realize that, having quit your job, you need to make something up. You tell her you got a raise.

"That's fantastic," she says.

"It's nothing big," you say. "I manage three people. It's just for this project, maybe, unless I do well. Then I might move on to a bigger project."

"I'm trying to figure out how excited I should be," she says.

"You know when Taco Bell brings back a burrito, and it was your second favorite thing on the menu?" She nods. "A tick below that."

She says she wishes she had made a cake. She's always looking for a reason to make cake.

Car
Cost: Low
Reliability: Medium
Chance of success: Low

2. Plane

Afraid of being seen by someone you know while hitching, you opt for a plane. You pay in cash, to diminish the paper trail. The ticket agent does a double take at cash and no bags. You get a feeling of dread in your stomach, an acid lagoon right below your navel.

The TSA doesn't even make you wait in line, grabbing you as soon as you get to security and escorting you to a private room. A man with the kind of hair cut bad guys have in seventies counterculture films comes in with a folder. It's red and has brackets on the end. You wonder how they could possibly have enough paperwork on you to warrant a folder.

He asks where your final destination is. You tell him you're not sure. Not here. He asks where you're going to stay. You tell him you don't even know where you'll be. He asks if you're travelling alone. Aren't we all? you say. He tells you to please just answer the question. Are you with anyone? You say no, not really. You live with someone. You sleep next to them at night. But are you with them? When you first got together, all these bits of your ego collided with bits of their ego, and it felt like you were working and growing and moving. Then you decided what restaurants you like, and you told them your life goals, and you figured out what they could actually help you with, and now you're moving in tandem. But the thing is, when you and everything around you is moving in this one direction, how is that any different from standing still? And how is standing still any different from being dead?

The TSA agent asks where you're going, and you realize he's doing the interrogation trick where they ask you a question over and over, to catch you in a lie. You tell him this was all a bad idea and ask, if you promise to never fly again, can you go? He tells you flying probably isn't going to be an option for you in the future. As you're leaving, you ask the agent if he likes you. As in, does he, personally, like you, as a person? He says no.

Your fiancé roasted a chicken with vegetables. The onions spent so long caramelizing that it's like chewing on taffy. After the meal, she brings out a homemade cake. It's red velvet with cream cheese frosting. It has a candle on it. She puts it in the middle of the table, and you wonder what would happen if you picked it up and threw it in her face. Would she scream? Or cry? Or laugh and fight back and it gets so loud the neighbors call the police and you'd answer the door in clothes hastily thrown on, frosting spiking up your hair?

No, you think, none of that would happen. She'd just get upset and read while you cleaned up.

The cake is delicious.

Plane
Cost: High
Reliability: High
Chance of success: Low

3. Boat

You've gone on picnics overlooking the bay but never actually been to the port. You're expecting some sort of dock situation, but it's just a lot of gates and guards who are surprisingly polite as they listen to you explain yourself and then ask you to leave. Out of sight of the gate, you walk off the road and stumble through bushes and gravel and find the fence, which is topped with razor wire. You walk along it, looking through at boats sitting at port. This is by far the most frustrated you've felt. The boats are right there, sitting idle. Isn't stowing away a thing? Or working for your passage? Wasn't that a proud naval tradition, or something?

A group of rough looking people in flannel and Carhartt were eating lunch at a metal picnic table, but they've all stopped and are staring at you staring at the boats. You wave. One of them yells something in what you think might be Mongol. It doesn't sound friendly. He walks over and, in broken English, asks if you got a problem. Yeah, you say, you're looking to get out of town. He asks if you have money. You say sure. He looks around, writes a number on the back of a card, and hands it to you. You leave and look for a payphone but give up after an hour and borrow a stranger's cell phone. You get a meeting for the next day.

"The project is going great," you tell your fiancé. Dinner is chicken thigh breaded in almond flour with squash, onion gravy, and melted cheese on the side. Autumn food, your fiancé calls it. "They're blown away by how much the team is getting done. They're talking about pulling me out early and seeing what I can do on a bigger project."

"Wow," she says, excited in a tired way. When you first met, she had an angular thinness that would snap into awkward when she got excited, like she hadn't quite grown out of being a girl made of elbows and crooked front teeth. Now she was forty pounds heavier, wore button up shirts with yoga pants, and had buried her awkwardness in polite excitement that was both transparent and infuriating. "That's so great. I feel like I'm running out of ways to celebrate."

"That's okay," you say, smiling back at her. "I'm tired anyway." You watch a movie and have sex. When she gets close to orgasm, her face goes slack and her jowls judder.

Boat
Cost: Low
Reliability: Low
Chance of success: Low

4. Smuggling

Sergei's office is in a warehouse bustling with men driving forklifts and yelling good natured insults at each other. When you tell him what you want, he seems baffled by the challenge of getting someone out of the city but also excited. He pulls out maps and converses with someone in Russian. There is a bandolier of grenades on a table. You suspect Sergei traffics prostitutes.

Eventually, he turns to you and asks if you'd be willing to work on a boat and not talk to anyone for ninety days. You tell him, yes, like a stow away, exactly. He brings out a barrel, a crate, and a stepping stool. You climb into the barrel, and he tries to get the lid on. To smuggle you on board, he says. Will I be able to breath? you ask. His English seems to fail him, though you suspect he's just ignoring you.

The lid is on the barrel but not secured when people start yelling outside. There's a loud crash and what sounds like those New Year's Eve blaster caps, which you realize are gunshots. Sergei stomps off. You decide to wait this one out in the barrel.

Several times over the next few minutes of gunfire, someone starts to scream and, with a pop, it is abruptly cut off. Soon, the Russian voices dwindle down to just Sergei's. While he yells at the cops that he will cut them up and feed them to his bear, you gently remove the lid of the barrel and look out. Sergei is crouching behind some crates at one end of the warehouse. He is holding a katana. You look at the other end of the warehouse and see a black-helmeted head poke out and yell at Sergei to come out, hands raised. Behind you is a door marked EXIT.

Sergei sees you. Blood is oozing from his leg. He looks at the bandolier of grenades and signals at you to throw it over. You shake your head. He points the katana at you and does this bark that is either Russian for "toss me the fucking grenades" or an exclamation of pure, animal rage. With a bit of difficulty, you get out of the barrel and, without looking back, sprint through the door behind you and out across a mercifully police-free yard.

Your fiancé comes home to find you laying on the futon, fully clothed plus a blanket, staring at the ceiling.

"Not feeling well?" she asks.

"I feel fantastic," you say.

She drops her fuchsia tote and feels your forehead. When you're sick, you love being taken care of, but you're embarrassed by liking it and go to extreme lengths to hide any symptoms. She knows this about you, like she knows everything about you. She goes to the kitchen, and when she comes back she has a cup of tea for you.

"Let's buy a house," you say. She laughs.

"You're definitely sick," she says.

"I'm sick of paying rent. I want to have a yard and a dog and do home renovation."

"We can talk about it later."

"No, let's talk about it now, and decide now, and decide to do it, now. And let's get married, too, tomorrow, at the courthouse."

She sits down, gaps appearing between the buttons of her dress shirt, showing the tank top underneath.

"I'm not comfortable making any decisions right now," she says.

You struggle up to a sitting position.

"Why wait?" you ask. "So we can keep our options open? That's just fear. Fuck being afraid. Fuck everything but just doing something."

She takes the cup out of your hands and sips it thoughtfully. "I'm not afraid," she tells you. "But I want to wait."

She gets up and goes to make dinner. It's taco night. You wear sombreros and fake moustaches.

Smuggling
Cost: High
Reliability: Low
Chance of success: Medium

5. Barrel

There's a knock on your door the next morning after your fiancé leaves for work. It's a couple of polite men in suits, one tall with a beard and one short with a Superman curl in his hair. Behind them is half a dozen men in all black, holding semi-automatic weapons and wearing helmets that say FBI on them. They don't introduce themselves.

The men take you to a grey, otherwise featureless building, to a room lit with fluorescents. They get you coffee that is fantastic, and you talk with Superman curl about French presses. Eventually, the tall man slams his hand down on the table and yells at you to tell them where Sergei is. You explain that you don't know, that you just met him, and that your business with him was in no way illegal. By the way, you say, somewhere in Sergei's warehouse is a duffel bag full of cash, which is actually your cash, and if they find it, you would appreciate getting it back. The tall man slaps the table again.

They question you for a few more hours. The coffee is almost chocolaty, but with this great acidic bite at the end that takes the heaviness away. You drink cup after cup until you get anxious and have trouble focusing.

The agents tell you that Sergei is a bad man, that he's probably after you whether or not you know anything. To kill me? you ask.

To chop you up and stick you in a barrel, they say, and ship you around the world, never showing up on a manifest, transferred forever between ships. It's how he hides bodies. So you'd get out of this town? you ask. Oh yeah, they say. If you don't let us help you, you'll be long gone.

Hmm, you say, sipping your coffee. Interesting.

They let you go late, and your fiancé is already in bed. Dinner is a cold feta and turkey burger with pickled salsa fresca. You eat it in front of your computer and read about shipping lanes.

Barrel
Cost: Low
Reliability: High (according to the FBI)
Chance of success: High

6. Abduction

The next morning, you open the door to a knock, ready for another day of questioning, an empty thermos in hand for some of that coffee. It's the mailman, or at least it's Sergei in a mailman's uniform, except whereas mailmen are usually holding a package, he's holding a gun.

Ushering you into the living room, he tells you he needs to both take a hostage and make sure you don't talk, so he's grabbing a rock and going nuts on two birds at once. He moves you through the backyard, over the fence, down an alley, and in to the trunk of a Lexus.

You nap some. You'd stayed up late last night, getting drunk.

You're woken by Sergei opening the trunk and asking if you have any dietary restrictions that would limit restaurants you can go to. You say no, but you'd prefer something local. He agrees. Chains are soulless, he says, shutting the trunk.

A while later, he opens the trunk, and you eat at a place on the side of the highway with brisket on the menu and plastic, checkered tablecloths. Both of you being hungry, you order the family sampler platter. He tells you to not worry about paying.

The conversation winds its way around to him murdering you. He tells you you seem calm about it. You shrug, trying to take a napkin out of the holder without getting BBQ sauce all over it. Isn't it funny? you ask. It's not like we aren't all dying all the time, it's just that as soon as you know how you're going to die, it becomes terrifying. So you're not scared? Sergei asks. Should I be begging? you ask. Should I grovel and tell you no, that I have a fiancé and I won't tell anyone? Sergei says that's a popular choice. You say sure, it's definitely a sensible option. And maybe later you'll change your mind and beg. But right now, you're enjoying tasty barbeque and a good conversation. That's all way more real than dying.

After, Sergei buys you some Dairy Queen and lets you sit in the passenger seat. Eating an Oreo Blast, going through plains lit by moonlight, semis floating past like pale ghosts, he tells you this is maybe the tenth time he's had to up and run away. He runs his hand over his buzz-cut head, the graying bristles making that scratching sound, the sound of exhaustion. He says when he was a student in Moscow, he was surviving on two hundred American dollars a year. he had a mattress, a tea kettle, a pot, a pan and a Bunsen burner. My neighbors were all prostitutes and drug dealers. A few nights a week, we would get together for a potluck of cabbage and beef, both boiled, salt and moonshine the only seasonings. I swore I would claw my way out of that poverty, and I have. But where am I going?

A safe house? you ask.

Yeah, he says. And then another city and another warehouse and hire more men who are clawing themselves to nowhere.

Abduction
Cost: Low (Sergei won't even take an IOU.)
Reliability: High
Chance of Success: Low

7. Forgetting
Over meals at local places, Sergei keeps telling you he's going to kill you. You eat at diners mostly, but also bistros, wine bars, pubs, and barbeque joints. Some are nicer restaurants, but you both have a passion for authenticity, which you agree is harder to find at higher end places. Sometimes he'll drive though a larger city, New York or Philadelphia, go through a Slavic looking neighborhood, sigh, and keep going.

You drive around for months. Eventually, you take up hiking together, to stay in shape. You talk a bit about the smuggling business. You have some ideas on how to improve his record keeping.

One night, you're at a campground on Lake Michigan, next to a group of college-aged women drinking and playing music. You feel too old for them, and Sergei is definitely too old, but he tells you to not kill buzz, goes over, and introduces himself. You end up drinking and getting high, and soon you, Sergei, and two women are skinny dipping. The water is warm, and there's a storm over Chicago in the distance. Every time lightning strikes, it gets mirrored in the lake, a double flash meeting in the sky scrapers of the city.

The women say it's beautiful, and you agree. Can you imagine being struck by lightning? you ask. A bolt reaching down, coming in through your head and going through you, touching places that have never seen light?

Uh, the women say, but then you'd be dead.

No, you say, that's wrong. The lightning would connect you to the clouds. It'd be an unbroken link between you and something miles high and long, bigger than you can even imagine. Everything would make sense. That's the opposite of dead.

Yes, Sergei says. It'd be beautiful.

You settle in Chicago. Sergei takes you to meetings with other Eastern European men and introduces you as his partner. He doesn't talk about killing you anymore. You build up a business together and go out to eat at new restaurants when they open up. Years go by. He tells you he trusts you completely and would you set up a business for him in Barcelona? Nothing too dangerous. It'd be a front for money laundering.

In Spain, you mostly keep to yourself, doing a lot of hiking and teaching yourself Spanish. Eventually, you talk to a woman over papayas at the market. She invites you over to her house for supper, and you meet her friends and make plans for the next weekend, and so on and so on. Soon, you get lonely when you hike by yourself.

One day, the woman is your wife. She cooks a lot of fish. You love her ceviche.

Forgetting
Cost: Low
Reliability: High
Chance of success: High

8. Nostalgia
You see her when your daughter is picking out cherries at the market. She's wearing a long, flowing, white dress, the kind

fortysomething women tourists always wear in Barcelona. Her son is picking out peaches.

Will you stare? Will you say hello, like you're happy to see her? Like you want to catch up?

You're surprised to find that you miss her. You remember sitting on the couch, watching TV, her body soft under your arm, her hair tickling your cheek. What was wrong with it, you can't remember anymore. It was life, wasn't it? It was all living.